The Red Bee: All the Rage

by Yoko Bongo

THE RED BEE: ALL THE RAGE

Chapter One: Gator Hole

The mosquitoes claimed her at mile marker 23.

They materialized from the sawgrass in a column forty feet high, a green-brown pillar of shifting wings. They did not move with the aimless, blood-hungry democracy of the glades. They surged with the calculated focus of a pilgrimage. This living helix bifurcated around Dale's rented Cybertruck, ignoring the sterile glass to focus on the heat of the woman within. Jenna Raleigh watched them in her side mirror and felt a sensation she had suppressed for eight years unfurl in her chest like an iron fist opening to reveal a tender, aching palm. It was the heavy burden of recognition. It was the weight of being remembered by the small and the many.

She kept the window down, her elbow resting on sun-baked metal. Sweat mapped its way down the collar of the linen blazer she'd purchased for a tenure review abandoned by the board before it could be conducted. The distinction mattered only to her, a ghost of a career she still clung to while the world outside chose entropy. The air conditioning had surrendered north of Orlando, a mechanical suicide that sensed her low threshold for disaster and offered her one more.

"—technically not my department," Dale's voice rattled through the Bluetooth. She endured the noise only because silence required more energy than endurance. "The ospreys first. Then the grackles. Now the marsh rabbits are changing. They aren't even birds, Jenna. Are you listening?"

She was watching an *Aedes* land on her forearm. It deployed its proboscis with the surgical precision of an assassin. Then it ceased. The insect bypassed the stunned stillness of a pesticide kill or mechanical failure; it became a statue of obsidian intent. It curled into a black question mark against her skin. A second followed. A third bit her, finding the vein, and Jenna felt a cold thread drawn through the meat of her bicep. Recognition traveled in one direction; she felt it return from the other. She crushed it. Her own red smeared the white linen, turning a professional garment into a piece of evidence.

“Show me,” she said, cutting through Dale's bureaucratic drone.

“Show you—”

“The site. The drainage point. The place your contractors fear to tread.” She was already calculating. The specimen kit was in her bag. The hard-shell case waited in her carry-on, compressed and hungry. “Show me what they ran from.”

⁂

Gator Hole existed only as a condition, a consensus of wrongness whispered by those who worked the fringes of the glades. No map dared to name it. The water moved with a heavy, oily purpose. It bore an iridescent sheen, a rainbow signature of something designed in a laboratory rather than spilled by accident.

Jenna stood on the embankment in ballet flats she had regretted since the airport. She watched Dale maintain a five-foot buffer from the vegetation, performing the theater of caution for an audience of one. The swarm ignored him. They orbited Jenna instead, a noisy, patient halo of wings. She read Dale’s lips through the vibration of the air.

“The samples come from there,” Dale said, pointing at a rust-orange pipe voiding fluid into the shallows. The rate of flow suggested active production. “Kennedy had three separate contractors refuse the site. The biotech firm out of Delaware just stopped answering emails.”

“BrinCell,” Jenna said. Her flats sank into the gray-green sludge. She remembered the twelve-thousand-dollar debt for her daughter's orthodontia, a predatory loan disguised as medical processing. She waded deeper into the mud, the mosquitoes parting for her like a dark wake. "A small ruling class for a small, dying world."

"Small world," Dale offered, a shallow platitude.

"Same thing." She crouched at the waterline. As she dipped the first vial, the fluid resisted for a microsecond—a hydraulic suspicion—before yielding. Beneath the surface, something moved against the current and then stopped, as if it had been seen. She capped the glass. "You didn't call me because of the birds, Dale."

"No."

"You called me because your contractors fled, and you need a paper trail proving this contamination is environmental. You need to protect your launch window. You also called me because you know I will answer." She filled the second vial. "I have apparently failed to learn better."

Dale said nothing. This was his version of honesty, a silence maintained while he occupied himself with his phone. He scrolled through the wreckage of social media while Jenna filled vials three through six. The mosquitoes shifted their frequency, a vibration transcending sound that settled in her ears. It was intention rendered into a low, thrumming frequency. *Here. This one. She will do.*

She capped the sixth vial and rose with a sudden, staggered motion. Forty-two years of human mileage and the erratic tides of perimenopause collided with a Florida heat that felt sentient, a heavy hand pressing against her sternum. Dale looked up, his face a map of dazed bewilderment. He had always been a man who preferred her features in the safety of stillness, unable to read the kinetic storm of her frustration.

"Jenna, I know we didn't end on—"

"The mosquitoes abandoned their instinct, Dale." She severed the air between them, refusing the tax of his sympathy. It required more of her than his negligence ever had. "They are coordinating. This isn't the hunger of a swarm or the mindless drift of a species. This is a unified intent. I have spent a lifetime documenting arthropod aggression, and this exists outside the known. When did this begin?"

"Two, maybe three weeks."

"And you sat on your hands until you needed a paper trail." She shoved the specimen kit into her bag, her thumb swiping through three frantic alerts from Ricky. Likely a lab safety lecture or a dispute over her timesheet. She turned toward the Corolla, the mosquitoes trailing her in a tight, disciplined formation. "Damn you for this, Dale."

He stayed rooted to the mud. Behind her, the electric whine of his Cybertruck rose—the sound of an expensive, sterile future manifesting as a hiss where an engine's heartbeat belonged.

"The Red Bee," he called out before she reached the door. His voice carried the practiced warmth of a man who knew exactly which lever to pull. "Come on, Jenna. You miss the sting."

She stopped. The sawgrass hissed in the wind. She did not turn.

"Your great-uncle broke ward bosses with trained insects," Dale said, stepping closer to the edge of the embankment. "You used to do the same with armor and a reservoir of rage that eight years of therapy couldn't drain. I am describing an evolutionary anomaly, and you are the only one with the blood to understand it. I am saying the Red Bee. I'm saying you."

"You are saying you need an expendable asset who still answers when her ex-husband whistles." She pulled the car door open.

The mosquitoes settled across her shoulders like a heavy, living mantle. "The answer is yes. That is the only shameful part of this."

She slid into the driver's seat. She refused to look at the hard-shell case in the back, its presence a practiced lie, compressed to look like mundane photography gear. She pushed down the memory of the seals, the cold grip of the exoskeleton, and the way the suit promised to swallow the chronic ache in her lower back—a debt her body had been collecting since she tried to become normal.

She summoned the ghost of Richard Raleigh. He had been Richard, never Rick. He prosecuted the rot of Superior City until the law proved too slow, eventually donning the red-and-yellow to hunt what the courts couldn't touch. He had died in a Pittsburgh steel mill in 1953, fighting Baron Blitzkrieg. He had fallen alone, yet his bees had kept the line, stinging until their tiny hearts failed. Her grandmother had framed it as a tragedy of a life wasted. Jenna, even as a girl, understood the truth. The swarm never surrendered.

The Launch View Motel sat at the jagged edge of I-95, offering a glimpse of the sky where the Kennedy Space Center occasionally bled fire into the clouds. Jenna showered with the door open, the specimen kit resting on the porcelain lid of the toilet. The vials unsettled her. The fluid within pulsed with a rhythm that defied physics, a pressure differential that made the plastic appear to expand and contract. They were breathing.

She was toweling her hair when the first insect breached the window screen.

Then the second. She stopped counting at thirty. They filled the small room in a dense, vibrating silence, coating the mirror in a mosaic of twitching wings. They clustered around the light fixture, their collective frequency humming in her marrow, making her molars ache. Jenna stood naked in the center of the room, recognizing the arrival for what it was. This was no infestation. It was a formal summons.

They wanted entrance. The suit was in the other room, out of reach.

The mosquitoes did not bite with random hunger. They sought the markers of her history—the shrapnel scar on her shoulder from a SHADE incendiary, the stretch marks of her pregnancy, the vulnerable dip of her spine. Bypassing the epidermis, they sought the ancestral ghost-code Richard had carried.

She felt the cold thread multiply, braiding itself into her nervous system. She collapsed into the bathtub before the first convulsion hit. She vomited black water flecked with silver that moved with a predatory intelligence before dispersing down the drain. When she wiped her mouth and looked in the mirror, the human Jenna had receded. Her sclera flooded a bruised red, her pupils narrowed to needles, and the bones of her face shifted into a sharp, hexagonal efficiency.

Her hands remained terrifyingly steady as she dialed Ricky. She should have been in shock, but her pulse was a rhythmic, calculated hum.

"Dr. Raleigh? I was just—"

"Ricky." Her voice was a layered harmonic, her own vocal cords vibrating in sympathy with a deeper, insectoid threat posture. "Do not call anyone. Not security. Not the CDC. And absolutely not Dale."

Silence. She could hear the boy's heart rate spike through the receiver. "You're in Florida," he said.

"I am in a primal kind of trouble." She watched a mosquito crawl along her forearm, reading the braille of her veins. "Look up BrinCell Data Systems. A Delaware shell. Biotech, peptide patents, financing. I need to know the owners. I need the bloodline of their money, and I need it yesterday."

"Dr. Raleigh, you sound... transformed."

"I sound like the consequence of a choice I didn't know I made."

Ricky Yamamoto was twenty-four, an idealist who believed that saving bees was the pinnacle of scientific endeavor. He had trusted her with his career, and she had spent two years shielding him from the compartmentalized wreckage of her past. She could hear him measuring the weight of her voice, the frequency that suggested she was no longer entirely the woman who had missed the safety webinar.

"You sound like you're becoming something," he whispered.

The observation hung in the static, a truth Jenna found she could not refute. She watched a heavy, obsidian tear track down the line of her jaw. It felt wrong—too viscous, too deliberate. The salt of her grief had been replaced by a black, oily discharge, a physical process occurring without her consent.

"Ricky. They knew I was the one. They weren't waiting for a generic host or some tangential metahuman biology. They waited for my DNA. My history." She stopped, a violent cough racking her frame. A silver filament, shimmering and alive, escaped her lips before she could swallow it back. "They were fishing with my great-uncle's ghost as bait. Whoever designed this understood the neurochemical lattice Richard Raleigh spent forty years weaving with his hives. They knew what that inheritance could carry."

"Richard Raleigh," Ricky said, the name sounding like an incantation. To him, it was a legend of the Freedom Fighters, a hero etched in monochrome. To Jenna, it was a heavy burden of genetic debt. "The original Red Bee."

"The original," she agreed, her knees hitting the carpet. She began to crawl toward the bedroom, her hands seeking the solidity of the floor while her mind drifted into a humming cloud. "He possessed a pheromonal sensitivity that defied the science of his era. He didn't just train those bees; he sang to them in a language of the nerves. My grandmother called it love. My father called it luck. I wrote the dissertation that mapped the pathway and watched an NIH review board bury it in a shallow grave in 2009."

"Someone exhumed it," Ricky said.

"Yes. Someone realized my research wasn't a theory, but a production manual."

The line crackled with a sudden, sharp interference. Ricky's voice thinned, stripped of its youthful bravado. "Are you suiting up?"

She looked at the hard-shell case. In the bathroom mirror, the red flood in her eyes had consumed the white entirely, the pupils narrowing into vertical slits. Her face had found a new, terrifying efficiency. "Not yet. I have to purge this silver from my lungs first. Then I need to map the link between my daughter's orthodontist and a drainage pipe in a Florida marsh. Then," she coughed again, the black water splattering the sink while the mosquitoes repositioned themselves with the calm practicality of a ritual audience, "then we'll see if the armor still knows my name."

"Dr. Raleigh—"

"Jenna. Call me Jenna." A laugh bubbled up, layered with an insectoid harmonic that made the bathroom fixtures vibrate. "If we're about to dismantle a biological weapons operation, we should probably dispense with the titles."

"We're not going to—"

"Look up BrinCell. Search the CDC's secure vaults for the word 'Hymenoptera.' There's a file from 2018 I was too tired to open because I was trying to pretend I was retired. Find out what happened to the three women who preceded me in this sequence."

"What three women?"

"The ones who came before. The knowledge is already here, Ricky, downloaded into my marrow." A cold shiver of borrowed intelligence rippled through her. "Don't come to Florida. Whatever happens next, stay clear—"

The call died. It didn't fade; it was severed by a cold, industrial hand. Jenna sat in the bathtub of the Launch View Motel, surrounded by a swarm that had ceased its hunger to simply witness her.

When the second wave of vomiting subsided, she stood. Her balance had shifted. She walked to the hard-shell case and initiated the sequence she had sworn to leave in the past. Biometric checks, joint lubrication, the hissing engagement of compression seals—the suit seemed to anticipate her movements, the original design expanding to meet the changes in her physiology. It was a dark communion. The armor settled over her, its exoskeleton swallowing the chronic ache in her spine. As the helmet sealed, the lenses didn't merely correct her vision; they translated the world into a grammar of heat, movement, and pheromonal trails.

She opened the motel door.

The parking lot was a void of asphalt, save for Dale's Cybertruck at the far end. Its cameras tracked her with a red, rhythmic pulse. Beyond the perimeter, I-95 flowed with a tide of travelers who remained blissfully ignorant of the chemical storm brewing in the sawgrass.

The mosquitoes rose in a single, consenting mass—a living cloak that draped over her shoulders. She activated the wings. The old hydraulics groaned under the weight of her new biology, and the battery level flickered at 73%. With a sudden, violent surge, she lifted from the ground, the force of the ascent shattering the sun-cracked pavement.

Forty-two years. Underpaid and overlooked. Now, something was singing in her blood, a reawakening in a register she was only beginning to master. The local bees answered. They weren't hers—not yet—but the wild colonies of the Florida scrub turned toward her signal with a wordless, ancestral recognition. They moved toward her in the dark, a loyal guard for a queen they hadn't seen in seventy years.

Richard had called them out of the air like a man calling a friend. She had always understood the science of it. She had never understood the terrible beauty of the feeling.

At 3:47 AM, the drainage pipe at Gator Hole continued its slow, toxic vomit. Jenna met the current in the dark. The suit's sensors hummed, filtering the fluid and returning a stream of data for Ricky's eventually-inevitable analysis: receptor-mimetic structures, unknown protein complexes, a biological signature that defied the suit's Freedom Fighters-era archives.

Then, the HUD flashed a single, cold line of text: PATENT PENDING.

The designation was a jagged blade in the dark. This wasn't an accident of evolution or a spill of industrial waste. It was a harvest. Someone had patented her bloodline before she even knew it was still flowing.

She launched a drone—a mechanical gnat, the skeletal ghost of Richard’s original design updated with modern, hungry sensors—into the throat of the pipe. It returned twice, bearing samples that defied gravity, clinging to the collection membrane like mercury with a grudge. She recorded every tremor. She logged the world with the obsessive precision of a prosecutor building a case against eternity. Richard had understood a truth lost to the neon-and-spandex crowd: the brawl was merely the overture. The true war lived in the documentation that survived the debris.

By the time the first bruised light of dawn licked the horizon, seventeen vials sat in her kit. The HUD's biometric overlay had ceased its frantic warnings. Her vital signs no longer registered as a series of errors; either the suit had surrendered to her new rhythm or her transformation had settled into a permanent, internal empire she would have to learn to rule. She stopped checking for Ricky's frantic follow-ups or the inevitable manipulative hooks from Dale. She even ignored the 4:13 AM ping from Kayla—a TikTok about the wreckage of generational trauma and mothers who prioritized the mission over the cradle. Jenna watched the video three times, the realization sinking in that it was a message written in the cipher of public shaming. She had been searching for evidence of her life, and her daughter had provided it.

She flew back to the Launch View low and slow, an aging engine conserving its remaining fire. Below, the morning traffic on I-95 began its mindless crawl. She allowed them to see her—the Red Bee, a relic dragged from the attic of the heroic age, eight years grayer and layered with an alien strangeness. She moved within a cloak of three wild colonies that had sworn fealty in the dark. Let the commuters aim their phone lenses. Let the algorithms churn her into content. A thought had taken root during the hours in the swamp: this contagion moved through attention. The pheromone didn't merely drift on the wind; it hitchhiked on the act of caring, on the neurochemical surrender to things that mattered. The careless were immune. The victims were those who still possessed something to lose.

She touched down on the motel roof, the landing jarring her teeth. She cracked the helmet seal and inhaled the Florida morning—a thick soup of rot, salt-spray blossoms, and the caustic ghost of rocket fuel from the Cape. She checked the digital static of her phone.

Dale: *Where are you? Contractors found something.*

Ricky: *BrinCell owns 14 shell companies. One of them funded your research grant in 2019. Dr. R, were you selected?*

Jenna's thumbs moved with a cold, rhythmic speed. To Ricky: *Selected for what purpose? Dig deeper.*

To Dale: *The contractors didn't find the source. The source found them. Tell them to stop breathing the air near that pipe if they value their lungs.*

To Kayla, after three drafts that she deleted like sins: *I'm in Florida. Your father's birds. I'm coming home Thursday.*

She had no idea if she was lying. She didn't know if the woman who stepped off a plane on Thursday would be the same woman who had left, or if the BrinCell vultures would pick her bones clean before then. But she sent the text anyway. She built the record. She made the case. She trusted that somewhere, in the vast, humming darkness of the hive, something would hear the plea.

The mosquitoes stirred, a restless shadow against the rising sun. The Cybertruck at the edge of the lot shifted its electronic gaze. Jenna sealed the helmet and dropped from the roof. She hit the asphalt with a bone-shaking thud, the suit's internal dampeners absorbing the impact that her forty-two-year-old frame could not. Standing before her was a woman in a BrinCell hazmat suit. The figure carried no collection tools, no scientific instruments. She carried only the heavy, bureaucratic weight of an ultimatum.

"Dr. Raleigh?" The voice was a filtered, synthetic warmth, the vocal equivalent of a corporate lobby. "You are experiencing a significant biological event. We have resources that can mitigate your distress."

Jenna looked at her own gauntleted hands. The hexagonal lattice had colonized her knuckles, visible through the outer shielding of the suit, a honeycomb rising from the meat of her hands. The transformation was announcing itself, a silent scream for recognition. She looked back at the corporate logo on the hazmat chest.

"I am experiencing clarity," Jenna said. "That is a state your resources can't touch."

She kicked off the ground and surged into the sky.

The suit's power failed at mile marker 31. She walked the final stretch to the motel, a solitary figure moving through a Florida morning that had suddenly turned liturgical. The light hit the sawgrass at angles that made the swamp look like a cathedral of consecrated glass. The distant, shimmering scaffolding of the Cape rose from the horizon—a monument to a future that had forgotten the ground. The mosquitoes walked with her, hovering at knee-height, a patient, local guard.

Back in her room, she plugged the suit into a stolen power strip and called Ricky. "BrinCell's collection team found me."

"They're ahead of us," Ricky said. He sounded like a man who had been awake since the dawn of time. "They know you're the apex. The protein in your samples—it's not a toxin. It's a key. It's keyed to a specific genetic sequence. This isn't a spill, Jenna. It's a harvest." She heard a sharp, intake of breath on the other end, the sound of a young mind shattering against a terrible pattern. "There are selection markers, Dr. R. The 'Hymenoptera' file... it's a list of criteria. Post-reproductive females. Metahumans with arthropod-adjacent physiology. Subjects with the neural circuitry of the Raleigh line."

"Richard Raleigh's blood," Jenna whispered.

A heavy silence followed.

"The original Red Bee," Ricky said, his voice a ghost. "They're farming a legacy. They need you angry. The pheromone replicates at a higher frequency under a stress response. It feeds on the pulse. They don't just want your cells; they want your fury."

Jenna looked at her hands, the honeycomb skin glowing beneath the motel's sickly yellow lights. "Then they've made a significant error in their investment. I have plenty to go around."

"The original," she whispered. "The man spent forty years stitching his own nerves into the hive, a slow-motion weaving of man and insect. He altered the very marrow of the Raleigh line, leaving a biological dormant seed that waited for the precise vibration to bloom." She coughed, a wet, rattling sound. She ignored the black bile staining her palm and filed the sensation away in a dark corner of her mind. "And now, the conditions are perfect."

"The three women who came before you," Ricky's voice was a thin thread of terror. "They're in the shadows of the file. Jenna—they were processed. Harvested like livestock. Tissue, spinal fluid, ovarian material. The death certificates claim 'natural causes,' but the timeline is a goddamn slaughterhouse schedule." He paused, his breath hitching. "They need you in a state of high-frequency distress. The pheromone thrives on adrenaline. It replicates with a predatory speed when you're activated. They don't just want your cells. They want your—"

"Rage," she finished for him. "They've bought the rights to my wrath." She looked at her hands, the hexagonal lattice of the transformation becoming the only truth her skin had left to tell. "Well, then. I suppose it's time they got a return on their investment."

"You aren't going to surrender to it?"

"I'm going to stop fighting it. I'm done with the immunosuppressants. I'm done dampening the fire I inherited from a man who died before I could ever know him." She coughed again, feeling a violent shift deep in her chest. A silver filament, slick and alive, escaped her lips. She watched it writhe for a second before letting it fall. "I intend to map every inch of this pipeline—from the filth in that drainage pipe to the boardroom where they're selling my blood. And then—"

"And then?"

Jenna thought of Kayla's digital ghost. The TikTok was a scream in the dark about mothers who chose the mission over the cradle, distance over presence, the cold necessity of war over the fragile comfort of a dinner table. She thought of Richard, who had made that same choice in 1953, dying alone in the sulfur and the heat of a steel mill, surrounded by nothing but the hum of his remaining swarm.

The bees had never stopped fighting.

"Then I'm going to find the true size of this shadow," she said. "I'm going to suit up and return to that hole. I want to see the face of what they're building before the hazmat ghouls come back to sedate me."

"Jenna, wait—"

"I'm sealing the helmet, Ricky. I'll call you when I've looked into the eye of the storm."

The helmet engaged with a pneumatic hiss, a finality that severed her from the mundane world. The mosquitoes rose with her, a living, pulsing cloak that answered the signal she was only beginning to master. The Florida morning broke around her—a humid, emerald expanse of rot and potential, a landscape designed to swallow the unwary. Jenna Raleigh let the fury rise, no longer a poison to be managed, but a compass. It was the only honest response to a world that had categorized her family's blood as a natural resource to be strip-mined.

The rental Corolla sat abandoned in the motel lot, a discarded shell full of professional blazers and the remnants of a woman who no longer existed. The Red Bee had returned. Whether this was the outcome anticipated by the architects at BrinCell or the ghosts at SHADE—the ones who had read her 2009 dissertation and seen a gold mine where she had seen a curse—remained to be seen.

She banked toward the marsh, a red-and-yellow streak against the bruised sky. She did not look back.

CHAPTER TWO: THE HIVE

Superior City University rose as a testament to the predatory weight of capital. It was a concrete husk, a brutalist scar on the skyline that once served as a Sears distribution center. Its transformation had been funded by a tech titan who eventually found his end in the crushing, silent dark of a submersible—a fact the campus ignored in print yet whispered through the cold, aggressive structure of the buildings. Entomology occupied the loading dock, an industrial byproduct relegated to the building's fringes. The steel door, seized by a humidity that strangled the city eight months of the year, required a ritual of force to open. Jenna's lab existed within the narrow confines of a former storage closet. A fume hood leaned sideways against a wall, a desperate installation born of misplaced optimism, and a solitary window offered a view of cinderblocks painted to mimic the texture of bark—a flat, mocking forest.

She had loved this sanctuary once. Now, she was trying to remember the rhythm of that affection.

Ricky was already waiting at 7:23 AM. His bicycle sat chained to the loading dock railing with four redundant locks, the visceral response of a man living in a city that rebranded itself as post-industrial without ever finishing the transition. Rain slicked his jacket, pooling on the linoleum in a dark mirror. He looked up, his features shifting through a sequence of silent calculations before settling into a rigid, defensive stillness. He knew the woman standing in the doorway was a different organism than the one who had left.

"Your flight was—" he began.

"Red-eye." Jenna didn't shed her coat. She placed her bag on the bench, the samples tucked into interior pockets like stolen relics. The Gator Hole kit sat wrapped in a thermal sleeve she'd fashioned from a motel laundry bag. "I need the hood. Now."

"Dr. Raleigh—"

"I'm not a threat to you, Ricky. But I need the exhaust."

She crossed the room in four strides. The black ichor she had been manufacturing since the motel bathroom had thickened during the flight, or perhaps her body had simply learned to contain the pressure. It surged against the back of her throat, an unrefined language seeking release. She leaned over the sink and let the darkness go. It moved down the drain in cohesive strands that resisted the water, a viscous silk that held its shape. The exhaust roared, sucking the floral, chemical scent of her own changing metabolism into the sky.

Ricky didn't flinch. He remained close enough to smell the change.

"That's expressed signal," Jenna said, wiping her mouth. She noticed the watermark of a hexagonal lattice appearing at her wrist, a faint ghost beneath the skin visible only under the harsh fluorescent hum. "An unknown variant. The suit's diagnostics identified the frequency but lacked a classification. I've been producing it since two AM. It pulses with my stress, but the baseline never drops to zero."

Ricky looked at the drain, then at her. "You need a medic."

"I need the mass spec and a window of silence." She shed the blazer she'd bought for a career that had stalled out—a garment belonging to a person she no longer recognized. The hard case at the bottom of her bag pulsed in her awareness. Since Florida, she could feel the presence of the suit, the pheromone weaving a sensory map of intentions and densities that rendered the room in high relief. "The Gator Hole samples are dying. The protein degrades at room temperature. I've been keeping them on the edge of viability, but the clock is fast."

She moved to the centrifuge, her blood going in first. She had taken the draws in the motel, six vials of evidence to determine if she was the victim or the vector. Ricky watched her with the focus he usually reserved for failing models. He offered recalibration rather than resistance.

“The birds in Florida were the bait,” he said.

“The lure. Dale’s bureaucratic panic was a script designed to ensure I was the one who answered the call. Someone understood the precise vibration required to pull me back to a drainage site without the proper shielding.” She paused, loading the first vial. “I thought I was being careful. They simply accounted for my caution.”

“BrinCell.”

“BrinCell is the husk. The intent lives inside.” She opened her laptop with a single, trembling finger, navigating the data she had mined during a layover in Atlanta. Sleeplessness had been her only companion. “I need the mass spec results before I voice my suspicions. I want your eyes to be clean.”

Ricky sat. Outside, the painted bark on the cinderblock wall shimmered under the rain, a pathetic simulation of life. Believing the lies mattered less than the maintenance of the pretense.

“You look different,” he said.

“I am different.”

“It’s the way you’re moving,” he insisted. He looked at her eyes—the Walgreens contacts she’d jammed in during a layover were pharmaceutical-grade, but they couldn't dampen the bruised red of the sclera. “The way you’re processing. You walked in and catalogued every leak in the ceiling and the residue in the hood without looking at them. You know my coffee is cold."

"Compound vision," she said. "The acuity is unchanged, but the coverage is total."

The silence that followed was heavy with the scent of ozone and wet wool.

"Does it hurt?" he asked.

Jenna felt the hexagonal pulse in her marrow. "Not anymore."

The mass spectrometer hummed, a mechanical witness delivering its verdict at 9:47 AM.

Jenna had spent the morning dissecting her own history. She ran three comparison sets against the frozen control samples—remnants of her pre-Florida life kept in the lab's backup unit like relics of a dead woman. The protein she hunted was absent from the old blood. It appeared as a ghost, a mere trace, in the first motel draw. In the second, taken after the swarm's arrival, it had reached a saturation that suggested colonization.

The Gator Hole samples provided the context. They were the source, the heavy water of this new, buzzing reality.

"Look at this," Jenna said. She didn't ask for his opinion; she was done with the theater of academic caution. The data was too massive to be viewed with anything resembling objectivity. She highlighted the sequence on the display—a long, elegant backbone of protein with receptor-binding regions anchored at every terminus. "Tell me what you see in the marrow of this."

Ricky leaned in, his forgotten coffee stone-cold on the bench. He possessed that rare focus where looking at a molecular diagram became a form of deep sight. He adjusted his jaw, a slight, rhythmic grinding of teeth.

"It's mimetic," he whispered. "These binding regions... they're keyed directly to the human limbic system. The amygdala. The anterior cingulate. It's a lock picking a door."

"Speak the purpose, Ricky."

"It amplifies salience. It takes whatever you're feeling and turns the volume until the speakers blow. It doesn't change the direction of the emotion; it just makes the signal impossible to ignore." He looked at her, his eyes wide with a realization that bordered on the spiritual. "This isn't a synthetic pharmaceutical. The backbone is biological. Someone took a natural pheromonal architecture and refined it into a weaponized strain. This began as something real."

"It began with my great-uncle," Jenna said.

She stated it with a terrifying lack of drama, the register of a woman who had already metabolized the horror. "Richard Raleigh spent forty years in a suit he built from a shoestring budget, but the real work happened in his nervous system. He didn't just train bees; he developed a neurochemical adaptation. He spoke to the swarm through a pheromonal vocabulary that science couldn't translate in 1950. After he died in that steel mill, the Freedom Fighters held his body for three hours. Long enough for SHADE to arrive and claim the remains."

She pulled up the next screen, the architecture of a betrayal she had been mapping since her layover in Atlanta.

"I wrote my dissertation on this pathway. I argued that the adaptation was hereditary—encoded into the germline, waiting for a trigger to activate in the next generation. The NIH buried that paper in 2009. They told me it was too speculative. But someone on that review board realized I hadn't written a thesis. I'd written a production manual."

"They used it as a recipe," Ricky breathed.

"A specification for a harvest." She opened the patent file she'd clawed out of the digital dark. "US2024/0089371A1. 'Compositions and Methods for Neurochemical Engagement.' The applicant is Meridian Biosystems. A Delaware shell. Meridian is a limb of a holding company called Palladian Research Partners. And Palladian is a subsidiary of BrinCell."

Ricky's fingers flew across his own keyboard. The names aligned on the screen like an executioner's list. "Jenna... Palladian also owns ClearPath Financing."

"My daughter's braces," she said. Her voice was flat, a cold stone. "Twelve thousand dollars to straighten Kayla's teeth, financed through a processor I thought was just another medical bloodsucker. They ensured a financial hook was in my jaw years ago. If I ever go public, they'll bury me in conflict-of-interest filings. They'll say I benefited from the very company I'm accusing."

She thought of the sleepless nights, the crushing weight of that debt.

"It was never just the money. ClearPath's app uses biometric authentication. Every time I made a payment, they were harvesting a heartrate, a palm-vein map, a keystroke profile. They weren't just collecting interest. They were building a stress profile. They were learning the exact rhythm of my anxiety so they could calibrate the trigger."

The word *farming* echoed in her mind, a relentless, buzzing mantra. They had been watching the crop grow for years.

"The patent," Ricky said, his voice trembling. "Can we find a way to block it? An inhibitor?"

"Merck is already ahead of us. They called the lab switchboard at 8:15 AM."

She watched him absorb the implications. The timing wasn't a coincidence; it was a choreography.

The call hadn't come through the usual channels. It was a direct line to a storage closet in a loading dock. The man on the other end had identified himself as a Vice President of Special Projects, his voice possessing the oily, frictionless confidence of a man who dealt in human commodities. He'd mentioned the *Hymenoptera File* before Jenna had even cleared her throat.

"They want me to consult," Jenna said, her eyes fixed on the mass spec readout. "They want the 'foundational subject' to help refine the antidote. They aren't offering a job. They're offering to let me help them package my own blood and sell it back to the world as a cure for a plague they started."

She looked at her hands. The hexagonal pattern was darker now, a map of the hive rising through the skin.

"They need me to be the face of the disease so they can be the hand that sells the medicine. They want my rage to be the marketing campaign."

The man's voice carried the sterile resonance of a legal briefing, every syllable filtered through a sieve of non-disclosure agreements and liability waivers. He spoke as if his vocal cords were managed by a board of directors.

"We understand the patent exists," he'd said, the sound frictionless and oily. "Our team is actively refining a receptor inhibitor. We anticipate a viable prototype within six to eight weeks, though progress remains tethered to the acquisition of biological data from a subject currently navigating the transition."

"From me," Jenna had replied.

"The compensation we're proposing is substantial, Dr. Raleigh. Consulting fees, primary authorship on the breakthrough, and public recognition as the foundational catalyst for—"

"You want to stitch my name onto a shroud woven from my own stolen cells. You want me to find validation in my own dissection." She watched a mosquito perish against the window glass, its life ending in a dark, wet smudge that the rain began to erase with indifferent rhythm. "Identify the origin of the patent. Tell me who provided the base compound before BrinCell began its refinements."

The silence that followed was heavy and curated. It was the pause of a man checking a script.

"I am not permitted to disclose—"

"Then your offer is an insult." She'd severed the connection, sitting in the sudden vacuum of the lab. The conversation had left a residue like ash in her mouth—the taste of being reduced to a yield, a biological resource to be harvested rather than a mind to be consulted.

Recounting the exchange to Ricky, she watched the realization sink into his marrow. This wasn't a reactive scramble; it was a symphony of extraction. The timeline for the cure had been established long before the first mosquito tasted the brackish water of Gator Hole.

"The antidote was waiting in a vault before the pathogen was even released," Ricky whispered.

"The profit was pre-ordained. The Rage Factor isn't the product; it's the liturgy of manufactured panic. It's the marketing campaign." She pulled up the ClearPath data, tracing the corporate bloodlines she'd mapped while suspended over the Georgia landscape. "This wasn't a localized spill. I have traces of similar seeding at six other sites within the Cape's weather radius. They've distributed a specialized *Aedes* variant across the entire dispersal range." She shifted to the next screen, the data points pulsing like a fever. "It's a pilot program. The compound goes live, the chaos blooms, the neurochemical engagement spikes, and then Merck—or whatever mask they choose to wear—steps into the light. They will sell the resolution at a premium to a population drowning in a sea of manufactured fury, desperate to feel a phantom version of peace."

"And you," Ricky said, his voice thinning. "The one it didn't just agitate."

"I am the visible edge case. The proof of concept that makes the threat feel tangible." She felt the pheromone stir in her chest, the cold thread braiding itself into a new, internal lattice. It was no longer a foreign presence; it was becoming a part of her own nervous system's terrain. "The Red Bee losing her mind. A relic of the Freedom Fighters going rogue. The spectacle of my transformation creates the urgency. I am the fear that drives the demand."

"You're the advertisement."

"I was cultivated for it." The realization sat in her gut like lead. She hadn't just been chosen; she had been farmed. "Richard's biology, refined through forty years of proximity to the hive, encoded into his very cells and passed down like a curse. I provided the dissertation that gave them the syntax for the harvest. I wrote the recipe, never imagining whose table it would serve."

Ricky remained silent for a long moment, the kind of pause that signaled his brain was connecting distant wires. "The holding company. Palladian Research Partners. I followed the thread through the 1947 filings."

"Show me."

He pivoted his monitor. The documents were ghosts of ink and bureaucracy, pulled from the digital archives of Delaware's SEC disclosures. Palladian was a limb of Sweetwater Holdings LLC, an entity birthed in 1947. Its registered agent was a ghost firm, long since dissolved, but the founding signatures remained.

Jenna stared at the scan. She knew that stroke of the pen. She had seen it in her grandmother's tattered scrapbooks, in the commemorative volumes of the Freedom Fighters that smelled of cedar and old grief. It was a signature from the official records of the wartime coalition, a name that belonged to the inner circle of the men who had stood beside Richard Raleigh in the final, desperate years of the conflict.

"That is a biological impossibility," she said. She didn't mean it as an expression of shock, but as a taxonomic observation. The signature shouldn't have been able to breathe in the modern world, yet there it was, an ancient hand reaching out from the foundation of the corporation that was now strip-mining her DNA.

"The signature is Uncle Sam's," Ricky whispered, his eyes wide.

Jenna looked at the document, the weight of a century pressing down on her. The embodiment of the national spirit hadn't faded into legend; he had incorporated.

"The personification of a nation's id doesn't die," Jenna said, her voice sounding like dry leaves. "He just finds a more efficient way to manage the assets. Plans within plans, Ricky. We aren't fighting a biotech firm. We're fighting the infrastructure of the country itself."

She looked at her hands, the hexagonal patterns becoming more pronounced, a map of the hive rising through her skin to greet the light.

"He was there when Richard died," she whispered. "He watched the bees continue when the man fell. He didn't see a tragedy. He saw a repeatable result."

Ricky's voice carried the jagged edge of a man who had seen a ghost in a high-resolution scan. "The biometric signature on the 1947 filing—it matches the Freedom Fighter archives. Every loop of the pen, every rhythmic pressure point. He had shed the skin of the propaganda poster to become the entity itself. The hand is the same. The vessel of the national id is the same."

Uncle Sam. He had bled beside Richard Raleigh, fought the shadows of the twentieth century, and stood witness when Richard's heart stopped in that Pittsburgh steel mill. Then, he had quietly traded his striped trousers for a corporate charter.

"SHADE didn't perish," Jenna said. The cold thread in her chest shivered, vibrating in sympathy with the revelation. The enemy of her family's bloodline had simply evolved, adopting the armor of limited liability and trading its uniforms for logos. "SHADE filed the paperwork to become the world's plumbing. And Uncle Sam—whatever that spirit becomes when it chooses dividends over liberty—is the one turning the valves."

Silence settled, heavy as wet wool. The rain drummed against the glass. The centrifuge whirred, a mechanical heartbeat in a room full of ghosts.

"The Freedom Fighters," Jenna whispered, her mind drifting to the faded photographs of Richard in his prime. Red and yellow. The Ray. Phantom Lady. They had fought to prevent a world of optimized control. Now, the entity built from Richard's marrow was selling mood-stabilizers to a population the Raleighs died to protect.

"Jenna—"

"I know." She walked to the sink. She twisted the tap, letting the hot water scald her palms. It was the only way to drown out the pheromone's rising frequency. The heat bit into her, grounding her to the meat and bone. "I know what they want. They need the fury. The pheromone is a fire that feeds on the pulse of the host. If I act out of outrage, if I become the spectacle they desire, I am just a cog in their marketing machine. I am the advertisement."

"Then how do you fight it?"

"I don't fight. I analyze. I dissect the undoing of this design. I will do the science, Ricky. I won't give them the performance of my anger."

It was a brutal discipline, a rewriting of her own soul.

At 2:17 PM, Ricky found the pulse. He had been mapping the spread since dawn, trying to reconcile the speed of the infection with the slow drift of mosquitoes. Insects follow the wind; this followed the light. He turned the screen toward her.

"It's the glass," she said.

"The electromagnetic spectrum of the screens," Ricky explained, his words rapid and visceral. "Social media interfaces. High-engagement triggers. The frequency activates the replication cycle in anyone already carrying the seed. It doesn't spread through the internet, but it grows there. It uses the dopamine hit—the surge of a like, the spike of a retweet—as a catalyst. It's an amplification vector."

"The angrier you are, the more you produce. The more you engage with the void, the faster the black water rises." Jenna felt the cold thread hum. It was a perfect trap. They had woven the contagion into the attention economy.

“Recurring revenue,” Jenna said, the words tasting of copper. “A product that exploits the very capacity to care. They took the human impulse to pay attention to what matters and turned it into a feedstock. They weaponized empathy.”

Ricky's jaw tightened. “The Hymenoptera file. The three women before you.”

“Yes. The test cases. The high-yield subjects.” Her voice was a razor. “We were the ones whose neurochemistry resonated most perfectly with the strain. The Raleigh descendants. The post-reproductive vessels. We aren't patients, Ricky. We are the crop.”

“And they died.”

“Average six months,” she said. The death certificates were lies written in the ink of convenience. Cardiac failure. Aneurysm. The system squeezed them until the pheromone burned through the host, then discarded the husks when the yield slowed. “The cycle is consumptive. It eats the person to produce the signal.”

She looked at her hands, where the hexagonal patterns pulsed in time with the lab's flickering lights.

“Then we have six months to kill the machine,” Ricky said.

“I have six months to become something the machine can’t digest,” Jenna replied.

“Becomes a natural cause,” Ricky said, the words falling like lead into the sterile silence.

“Yes.”

The fume hood hummed, a persistent mechanical drone against the glass. Outside, the rain had lost its fury, settling into a rhythmic, gray persistence. Within the containment vessel on the bench, the Gator Hole samples shifted. They moved with a collective pulse, a colonial intelligence that lacked a singular mind yet thrived through a shared, dark intention. Jenna had spent her life decoding the choreography of the hive, the way a thousand small wills could forge a single, terrifying purpose. These were not bees, yet they spoke the same grammar of the swarm. They were something altogether more ancient and more hungry.

"Someone knew about the Hymenoptera file before I touched it," Jenna said, her eyes fixed on the shifting fluid. "Someone tried to scream it through the proper channels and was silenced with surgical precision. They stripped him of his boards, his committees, and his advisory roles. They eroded him until there was nothing left but his name." She pulled up the dossier, the digital record of a slow-motion institutional execution. "Now he lives in a Faraday-caged basement in Bethesda, whispering through channels the digital world has forgotten."

"Who?"

"Dr. Ellison Webb. SHADE's chief biological consultant until 2003. He produced a classified report on the weaponization of metahuman biological inheritance—extracting profit from the very blood of the extraordinary. They buried the report beneath a clearance level he didn't possess. In 2009, the year my own work was shoved into a drawer, they cut him loose. He sent a memo in 2018. I ignored it. I was busy trying to be a ghost."

"You think he's still breathing."

"I think the system prefers containment to elimination. Murder creates martyrs and investigations; containment creates irrelevance. Webb is an old secret kept in a dark room. They've harvested his silence for twenty years." She began packing the vials, selecting the data that would survive the journey. "I'm going to reach out. But I won't use a screen. I won't use anything that passes through the nerves of Sweetwater or their subsidiaries."

"Meaning?"

"Meaning I am going to use ink and parchment," she said, the irony lost in the gravity of her voice. "A physical letter. A PO box in Bethesda that's been active since 2004. He's been waiting for a reason to check it."

Ricky watched her, his expression a mixture of awe and dawning dread. "You've been mapping this out since Florida."

"I've been mapping it out since 2009," she replied. "I just didn't have the eyes to see the route until now."

⁂

She dialed Kayla at 4:30 PM.

The phone rang with a hollow, rhythmic persistence. Five times. Then the digital void of voicemail. Jenna had expected this, had rehearsed the words since the moment she'd seen the TikTok. Kayla's video was a jagged piece of glass, a testimony to a mother who chose the mission over the cradle. The timestamp—4 AM—meant her daughter had been awake, drowning in the thought of her. Jenna felt the visceral nature of the pain but refused to perform it. The system fed on maternal suffering; she would not offer it another calorie of engagement.

"Hey." Her voice was a layered thing, a second harmonic vibrating beneath her vocal cords. The pheromone was coloring her speech, a frequency the microphone would record and Kayla would feel in the marrow of her bones. She had tried to suppress it, but the effort was a fool's errand. Honesty was the only currency she had left. "I'm back. Florida is... a puzzle I'm still solving. I want to talk when you're ready. No theories, no missions. I just need to hear your pulse through the line."

She ended the call and placed the phone face-down on the bench. She refused to wait for the ring. That waiting was a form of neurochemical surrender, a bait for the pheromone to feed on her uncertainty.

She submerged herself in the work.

The analysis ran until the sun surrendered to the city's artificial glow. Ricky left at 8:00 PM, his silhouette disappearing into the rain after she'd promised him she wasn't in immediate danger. He biked home behind four locks, a boy trying to survive a war of giants. Jenna sat alone in her storage-closet kingdom, allowing the mask to slip.

The pheromone was a rising tide, rhythmic and inexorable. It wasn't the violent surge of the motel; it was the slow, structural encroaching of a new reality. She felt the skin of her upper arms tighten, a reorganization of tissue that felt less like an ache and more like a metamorphosis. Her body was redrawing its own blueprint. Across the lab, the samples in the containment vessel hummed—a frequency that settled in her teeth. It was a colonial signal, a language she was no longer merely observing, but becoming. The distinction between the researcher and the specimen was dissolving in the dark.

She thought of her great uncle.

She looked past the uniformed propaganda of the Freedom Fighters volumes, past the sepia-toned icon shaking hands with Presidents and the hollow commemorations. The Richard she knew lived in her grandmother's kitchen stories, a private archive of unspoken truths that escaped the digital dragnet. This was a man of the shadows, someone who wrote in a shorthand that looked like bird tracks to baffle the inquisitive. He grew his own herbs, a quiet rebellion against the eyes of commercial suppliers. He understood in the 1940s a truth that would take the rest of the world eighty years to learn: the systems of ordinary life are the channels of absolute control, and the distance between liberty and bondage is merely a matter of who holds the remote.

Richard had kept bees out of love, a genuine affection that demanded his full attention. The adaptation was the harvest of that care—the delicate neuro-malleability produced by decades of sustained focus, a slow-motion fusion between a human nervous system and the collective mind of *Apis mellifera*.

She had inherited this ancient, humming pathway. She had dissected it in her studies without realizing she was mapping her own marrow. And someone—Webb, or the shadowed entities he tried to warn in 2003—had found her dissertation and recognized a production manual. They saw that the delicate bond her great-uncle had forged through devotion could be strip-mined, refined, and deployed as a commodity.

The fume hood's mechanical roar was the only thing anchoring her to the present. She reached out and cut the power. The ensuing silence of the lab was heavy, a thick medium where the sounds of the city transmuted into data. Delivery trucks, distant sirens, the groaning groan of the former Sears distribution center as it settled into its bones—she heard the negotiation between old concrete and new renovations as a molecular friction.

She resisted the rage. She felt the pheromone pulsing in her blood, beckoning her toward that high-yield state of fury, the productive frenzy the system designed her to inhabit. She was a feedstock. She knew this. Instead, she chose the cold, deliberate burn of method. She would be the researcher who reclaimed her own body.

She began the letter to Webb.

She bypassed the digital void, opting for the tactile truth of paper. She found a pen in her desk, buried beneath a heating pad. She plugged the pad in and pressed it against her lower back, honoring the honest ache of her forty-two-year-old frame. It was a warm, persistent pulse, a small piece of the world that belonged entirely to her.

Dr. Webb, she wrote. *You sent a memo to the NIH in 2018 regarding a classified file labeled Hymenoptera. You signed your name to it, an act that signaled either a desperate need to be found or a total surrender to your containment. I am writing because the file has located me. I am Richard Raleigh's great-niece. I have inhabited this adaptation for sixty hours. I possess seventeen vials of the compound from the primary seeding site and three sets of blood-work documenting my own transformation. I have the patent filings and a corporate genealogy that leads back to the entity you fled in 2003.*

She paused, reading the words. They were stark and verifiable.

The three women who preceded me were consumed by 'natural causes.' I intend to decipher that euphemism before my own timeline expires. If you are willing to trade what you know for what I have, I am listening. If you choose silence, I understand. Six months is a narrow window to build trust.

She signed her name. The ballpoint pen began to fail, the last numbers of the zip code fading into a ghostly impression—a physical reality that no algorithm could simulate.

She sealed the envelope.

The samples in the containment vessel shifted in the dark, a patient, colonial movement. They communicated through a network of interdependencies, a collective existence devoid of individual will. She had once found this beautiful. Now, that beauty was a jagged thing, a structure where grace and lethality were one and the same.

Her phone vibrated on the desk. A text from Kayla. Three-short-one-long. The code of their history.

I got your message. You sound different. Call me Thursday if you can.

She read it three times. The third time, she allowed herself to feel the warmth it ignited—a visceral heat that was hers alone, something the pheromone could not harvest or refine into a product. It was the simple, messy love of a daughter for a difficult mother. She let that feeling pulse for twenty seconds, documenting nothing.

Then she hid the phone in her drawer and killed the lights. She sat in the darkness with her heating pad and her compound eyes, watching the world through a new, fractured lens. She thought of Richard, keeping Michael in his belt buckle, writing his secret files, trusting that a record of the truth would eventually find its mark.

She would build the case. She would document the crime.

She was also going to be much angrier than Richard had ever been allowed to be. That was the inheritance she claimed.

Chapter Three: The Expert

The package arrived before the dawn.

Ricky found it leaning against the loading dock's rusted steel teeth at half-past six. It was a padded envelope, its surface an anonymous skin devoid of postage or return address. Jenna's name was written in a hand that suggested ancient, rigid muscle—strokes that looked less like writing and more like incisions. Ricky had left it on her bench, untouched. Two years in the orbit of Jenna Raleigh had taught him the gravity of her boundaries. He felt the weight of it, a density that suggested a secret he lacked the clearance to name.

Jenna paused in the doorway, her compound vision layering the envelope's thermal shadow over its physical form. She crossed the room and gloved her hands—a reflex that had evolved into a survival instinct since Florida. Inside lay a burner phone, its battery fully charged, its digital slate wiped clean save for a single ghost in the contacts: BEEKEEPER. Below it, a scrap of paper bore two lines of that same surgical script.

Finally, she pulled out a black-and-white photograph. It was a photocopy of a memory. The man in the frame was younger, draped in the sharp, pressed violence of a 1940s military uniform. He was a face from her grandmother's attic, a figure that had flickered in the periphery of history from 1942 until 1953 before vanishing into the classified fog. Richard Raleigh stood beside him. The man's hand rested on Richard's shoulder—not the heavy palm of a commander, but the touch of a peer who had navigated the geography of the trenches and found themselves, miraculously, still breathing. He was tall, gaunt, wearing the American flag as if the stars and stripes were a second dermis grafted to his skeleton.

She knew this entity. He was the ghost in the machine she had unearthed in the corporate genealogy—the biometric signature that proved SHADE had never been dismantled. It had merely shed its uniform for the invisibility of the LLC. This pale titan had stood by while her great-uncle died. He had been positioned to arrest the descent and had chosen the role of witness. Then, he had harvested the remains to build a financial empire on the ruins of a hero's marrow.

Jenna gripped the burner phone. She walked to the window, staring at the painted cinderblock bark—the university's pathetic mimicry of a forest—and dialed the only number.

The line connected on the first pulse.

"Dr. Raleigh." The voice lacked the theatrical thunder of a myth made flesh. It arrived instead with the dry, rasping weight of an antiquity that had spent decades breathing the dust of its own burial. "You are on day three."

"Day three of what?"

"The progression. Seventy-two hours since the initial bonding. Your eyes have fully transitioned into their new efficiency. Your pheromone output has surged to four hundred percent of the baseline. You are operating on two hours of sleep, buoyed by a chemical mimicry of productivity that masks the debt your organs are accruing." A pause. Jenna felt the vibration of the voice in her teeth. "You have begun soaking your hands in hot water to dull the itch of the hexagonal bloom."

"How are you watching me?"

"I am not watching. I am remembering. The three who preceded you followed this identical choreography. The soaking will fail by day fourteen. The production rate will outpace the heat, and you will require a more radical management framework." Another silence followed, heavy with the texture of a man weighing the value of a secret. "I am not your adversary, Dr. Raleigh. Accept that truth before we continue."

"You built an empire on my great-uncle's corpse," Jenna said.

"SHADE did. I was a child of seventeen in 1947. I was not part of the internal structure until 1989." The voice remained level, drained of defensiveness. It carried the exhausted patience of a man who had lived with his own indictment for half a century. "I spent fourteen years within the heart of the system that engineered this. I walked away in 2003. I have spent two decades waiting for a descendant with the biological stamina to survive the trigger. Your letter and this phone crossed paths in the dark. We have reached the same conclusion at the same moment."

Jenna looked at the photo. At the younger man, his hand on Richard's shoulder in a year when they were still fighting the monsters that would eventually become their board of directors.

"Tell me about the three before me," she said.

The voice identified itself simply as Webb. He offered it as a tactical necessity, a way to strip away the mythology of the flag for the sake of the work.

"Dr. Sarah Chen," Webb said. The sound of turning paper echoed through the line. "Portland, Oregon. An entomologist of the old school. She was sixty-one when they found her. In a previous life, she had moved through the shadows as Queen Bee—regional work, the Pacific Northwest. She retired when her husband died, the same year your own life fractured. The selection criteria are precise, Dr. Raleigh. They target women at the intersection of expertise and isolation. BrinCell mapped her through her publications and a lineage that traced back to a woman in 1910—a woman who lived in the shadow of a courier for the Freedom Fighters. Even then, the bees knew the courier's destination before he spoke it."

Jenna felt the cold thread in her chest pull taut. The breeding program was older than she had dared to imagine. It wasn't an accident of biotech; it was a long-game harvest of a bloodline.

“Richard operated as an unintentional gardener,” Webb’s voice rasped, the sound of ancient parchment rubbing together in a dark room. “He spent forty years humming a melody to the hive, never realizing the world was beginning to vibrate in sympathy. His bees spoke to his allies, stitching a language into the biology of everyone he trusted. You and Chen and the others aren't merely a bloodline; you are a resonance. Richard tuned a generation to a specific biological register, an epigenetic haunting that sleeps in the marrow until the environmental pressure becomes too heavy to ignore.”

“And BrinCell found the frequency,” Jenna said, watching the rain smudge the bark-painted cinderblocks.

“SHADE located the maps in the ruins of 1947. BrinCell inherited the blueprint in 2003, once I took my secrets and fled. They waited for the infrastructure to catch up to their ambition. Sarah Chen was the pilot, the first seed planted in a community garden in Portland. They fed her the compound through the city’s veins in 2019. She called me seven weeks into her transformation, drowning in a terror she couldn't name, begging for a sanctuary I didn't have the power to offer.”

“You left her to the wolves.”

“I am a ghost in a Faraday cage, Jenna. My existence is a mathematical equation—I am worth more alive and silent than dead and investigated. Attention is the only currency they refuse to waste. I couldn't save her, so I gave her data. I gave her the anatomy of her own destruction. She lasted eight months. The compound metabolizes the soul; it converts the neurochemical exhaust of your emotions into a commercial harvest. Fear is a high-metabolic fuel. Sarah Chen burned through her biological reserves until her heart simply surrendered. The death certificate called it failure. I call it a finished harvest."

Jenna gripped the edge of the sink. She thought of the hot water she'd used to numb the itching hexagonal patterns on her skin, a small, desperate ritual that felt more like a prayer than a treatment. The porcelain was cold. The ache was winning.

"Amara Okafor followed," Webb continued, the sound of shifting paper marking the movement of a new file. "Lagos, 2021. A biochemist who thought she could hide her nature behind academic citations. BrinCell read the subtext of her research on colony communication and found the direct pheromonal sensitivity she'd tried to bury. They poisoned her through a water treatment contract. She contacted me at nine weeks, but she didn't beg. She calculated. She tried to negotiate her cooperation for an inhibitor, playing a game of chess with a system that had already mapped every move. Calculation is the highest-yield state for the Okafor variant. The pheromone thrives on strategic threat assessment; it ran her nervous system like a high-performance engine for six months until her brain bled out. Cerebrovascular event. She was fifty-three."

The room felt smaller, the air thick with the ghosts of women who had tried to think or feel their way out of a biological trap.

"Dr. Yuki Tanaka," Jenna whispered. She spoke the name to anchor it to the world, a ritual of acknowledgment for the fallen.

"Sapporo," Webb said, his voice thinning into something like reverence. "A theoretical biologist with a quiet life and a grandmother who had been Richard's silent correspondent in the fifties. Richard wrote to her about the hive the way a man writes to his only mirror. Yuki breathed the compound in her own laboratory, hidden in the reagent stocks of a research grant funded by a Palladian shell. She lasted fourteen months. She was different—quiet, resigned. She used her own tools to build a perfect model of her expiration. She didn't ask for a cage or a cure. She simply asked to not be a solitary figure when the lights went out."

Jenna closed her eyes, feeling the pulse of the samples on her bench, a colonial thrumming in her blood.

"She died in March of 2022," Webb said. "The death certificate—"

"Stop." The word fell like a blade, flat and devoid of the harmonic distortion that usually frayed the edges of her voice. No buzzing. No vibration. Just the unvarnished grit of a woman demanding the truth. "Before you finish that sentence, tell me about Tanaka."

A pause echoed from the Maryland basement. "Very well."

"The three of them—Chen, Okafor, Tanaka. Did you witness their ends? Did you see the meat and bone of them in the cold, or are you just reciting the ledger?"

The silence that followed was a three-second void. Jenna counted every tick.

"No," Webb admitted.

"The death certificates were filed. The cases were closed. But the bodies—"

"I accepted the documentation because it was consistent," Webb's voice shifted, an alert frequency waking in the static. He was no longer just an observer; he was a man scenting a shift in the wind. "You've unearthed a fracture in the record."

"My lab assistant has been dissecting the corporate genealogy. He found a discrepancy in the Sapporo filing. The medical examiner who signed Tanaka's death certificate had his license suspended six months prior. It was reinstated three weeks after the ink dried. A quiet, administrative ghost-dance." She paused, feeling the cold thread in her chest pulse. "He also found a payment. Three months after she was supposedly in the ground, a Palladian subsidiary sent funds to a private facility in Hokkaido. The line item was 'ongoing subject maintenance.'"

Another three-second hole in the conversation.

"Subject maintenance," Webb whispered.

"That is the designation for a resource," Jenna said.

"Then she remains in the light," Webb's voice shed its exhausted patience, replaced by a jagged, hungry energy. The trajectory of his twenty-year exile had just been rerouted. "If Tanaka is alive, she is not a prisoner. She is a template. The late-stage synthesis Merck and BrinCell are chasing—it requires a viable biological substrate. You cannot synthesize the completion of the cycle from a dead culture. You need the living engine."

"They need someone who survived the six-month burnout," Jenna said. "Someone who didn't collapse, but finished the transformation."

She let the realization settle into her marrow. Her compound eyes watched the morning light filter through the window, refracting into a myriad of shifting data points. Beneath the tactical assessment, she felt a cold, human clarity. If Yuki Tanaka was in Hokkaido, she hadn't been rescued. She was being kept. A captive lung breathing out profit.

"Who runs the harvest?" Jenna asked. "The man with the pipette, not the man with the title."

⁂

His name was Valentin Stinkov. Webb delivered the file in doses, a measured administration of a toxic history.

Stinkov was a relic of the FSB's Special Technical Operations, a biochemist who had spent decades in the shadows of Soviet programs exploring the militarization of the hive. When the state abandoned the research as unprofitable, Stinkov took the secrets for himself. He had been purged in 2014 for unauthorized trials on his own people—human hives built in secret. In 2018, the entities behind Sweetwater Holdings bought his loyalty. By 2019, he was planting the seeds in Sarah Chen's garden.

"He is a master of the hunt," Webb said. The word was heavy with a grudging respect. "The FSB taught him to map the landscape for the most vulnerable targets. He looks for the transition points—the post-career, post-reproductive windows where the neurochemical terrain is most fertile for the initial bonding. He doesn't hunt the people; he designs the conditions that compel them to come to him."

"The birds," Jenna said. "The crisis Dale served up. The entire lure."

"Stinkov mapped the seeding sites based on the Cape's flight paths. He knew the environmental fallout would trigger a bureaucratic reflex, and he knew your credentials made you the inevitable choice for the task. He has been studying your output since 2009. He read your dissertation when the NIH was still burying it. He has spent fifteen years building a cage shaped precisely like your life."

She thought of the column of mosquitoes at Gator Hole, a forty-foot helix of waiting intent. It hadn't been a random encounter; it was a reunion. The compound hadn't just found her; it had recognized her.

"He documents the process," she said. "Online. In the dark corners where grievances bloom."

"He craves the recognition the Academy denied him. Since 2020, he has been using the forums as a secondary vector. He finds the reactive, the isolated, the people whose internal friction is already high. He seeds these digital hives with modified variants, harvests the behavioral data, and funnels the results to the Sweetwater board. It isn't a hobby, Jenna. It's a distributed clinical trial where the subjects pay with their own sanity."

Jenna remembered the threads she'd scanned—the bitter, translated syntax of a man who viewed the world as a laboratory for his own resentment.

"He hates women," she said. "It's the primary bias of his research."

"He believes post-reproductive women are the optimal vessels for the pheromone's growth, yet he holds the vessels in contempt. The two ideas coexist in his mind without friction. The contempt is part of the method—he believes a subject that is dismissed is easier to harvest." A pause. "He was wrong about you. He assumed your anger would be a consumptive fire, like Chen's or Okafor's. He didn't account for the nature of your focus."

"And what is that?"

"You are angry about the truth," Webb said. "That makes the signal too clean for him to manage."

Jenna looked at her hands, the hexagonal watermark glowing in the dim lab light. The rage was there, but it wasn't a fire. It was a map.

"He views the post-reproductive female as a fertile substrate for extraction, a biological factory that is simultaneously essential and beneath regard. To him, those positions aren't at odds. The contempt acts as a shroud; it's easier to harvest a resource you've already decided is invisible." Webb's voice crackled, a dry harvest of sound. "He miscalculated your fire, Jenna. He anticipated the panicked heat of Sarah Chen or the cold, doomed arithmetic of Amara Okafor—burn-off that eventually consumes the engine. He failed to see the composition of your rage."

"And what do you see?"

"I see an anger with a syntax," Webb said, his words measured as a ritual. "It possesses a target and a grammar. This isn't the chaotic pulse of a wounded ego or the static of a frustrated negotiation. It's the product of a terrible understanding. Stinkov needs his subjects to rot from the inside out, fueled by their own sense of loss. Your rage isn't about yourself. It's about the machine."

Jenna leaned against the cool glass. Outside, the rain had surrendered to a pervasive mist, a gray suspension that blurred the lines of the world until Superior City became more of an idea than a geography.

"I'm coming to Bethesda," she said.

"Yes."

"Not for sanctuary. I need the bones of the operation. I want the Sweetwater archive from 2003. Everything you carried out when the lights went dark."

"I carried out the world," Webb said. The exhausted patience in his tone shifted, acquiring a new, load-bearing density. "I have sat in this dark for twenty years waiting for a pair of eyes that could actually see the record. I have been waiting for you."

"Tanaka," she whispered. "If they're keeping her breathing..."

"The Hokkaido facility is the likely lung. We must confirm the site. If she has reached the later-stage production, she's no longer just a subject. She's the template. Merck is racing for an emergency authorization—six to eight weeks until the launch."

"That's a deadline for the shareholders," Jenna said. "It doesn't concern me."

"It should. It marks the moment the theft becomes a legacy. It's the threshold where the blood of your great-uncle and four discarded women is laundered into a pharmaceutical brand. Once the marketing campaign starts, the truth becomes a nuisance to be legislated out of existence."

Jenna turned the photograph over on her bench. Richard stood there, his hand held with that strange, instinctive looseness, giving the ghost in his belt buckle room to breathe. Beside him stood the man who was now a voice in a Faraday cage—Uncle Sam, the spirit of a nation that had decided to incorporate.

"Three days," she said. "I have work to finish here. Then I move."

"Three days. Avoid the trains; the facial recognition at the gates is keyed to the federal dragnet. Take the bus. Pay in cash. Bring the samples." A sharp, indrawn breath. "And bring the suit. It's the only part of Richard they couldn't patent."

She severed the connection. The burner phone went into the drawer, resting beside the heating pad like a dormant insect. She stood by the window, staring at the artificial forest painted onto the cinderblocks. She thought of her grandmother's kitchen, the smell of old paper and the quiet, heavy grief that had always been kept face-up. Her grandmother never hid the dead; she gave them the dignity of being seen.

Jenna turned the photograph face-up on the bench and submerged herself in the data.

At noon, the trap snapped shut.

Ricky hadn't been hunting for the thread, but his monitoring of the digital undercurrents had snagged a keyword cluster that shouldn't have been there. He flagged a post at 11:47 AM that used her name with a casual, clinical cruelty. Jenna stood over his shoulder, her compound vision slicing through the screen's refresh rate. She could read the electromagnetic residue of the interaction, a greasy film of intent that lingered on the pixels.

The post was a fractured English mess, the syntax of a man who had learned the language from a technical manual and the gutter of the internet. *Raleigh subject day three confirmed activation. Gator deployment successful. Variant 4.7 producing above projection. The Bee Queen comes again lol. We are very patient.*

Pinned beneath it was a molecular diagram. Jenna felt the pheromone surge in her marrow—a cold, silver thread of readiness that her body now recognized as a precursor to conflict. She breathed through the hum, watching the sensation crest and recede. She observed it as she would a hive, noting the intensity without surrendering to the swarm.

The diagram was a map of her own becoming. It was a simplified rendering of the compound's structure, but it included a synthesis pathway she hadn't seen in the patent. It was an extra step in the chemical choreography, a mutation in the dance that suggested the transformation didn't stop at the skin. It was building toward a new expression.

She stared at the image, her pupils narrowing to needles. The machine wasn't just changing her eyes; it was preparing a harvest she hadn't yet named.

"Don't reply," Ricky whispered, his voice small in the sterile air.

"I know."

"I'm serious, Jenna. He's fishing. He wants the engagement. He wants the stress response to feed the replication."

"I am aware of the vector." She straightened, her spine cracking with a sound like dry wood. The rage was there, a steady, cooling reservoir. "He's showing his work to his community of the aggrieved. He's reporting his yield. But he just gave me the one thing he shouldn't have."

"What's that?"

"The synthesis protocol. He thinks I'm the experiment, but I'm the only one in the room who actually understands the biology." She walked to the sink and ran the water over her wrists, the heat grounding her. "He thinks he's writing a story. I'm going to make sure it's an autopsy."

"Don't reply," Ricky said, his eyes anchored to the glow of his screen.

"I know."

"I know you know. I say it because the silence of caution is free, while the cost of a single keystroke is a debt we cannot settle."

"I know, Ricky."

Jenna moved to the sink. She twisted the cheap faucet, letting the hot water scald her palms against the porcelain. She had forgotten the sensation of cold; her nerves now interpreted temperature as a variation of pressure, a different kind of weight. For thirty seconds, she watched the steam rise, thinking of Stinkov in his distant, sanitized cage. He would be watching his metrics, waiting for the ripple of her reaction to validate his work. Silence was a variable in his equation. Restraint functioned as its own form of data. In this ecology of extraction, every hesitation was a heartbeat he could measure.

She cut the water and dried her hands with a clinical, heavy deliberate.

"The new production pathway," she said, nodding toward the diagram. "The architecture he left out of the patent."

"I'm running the models now." Ricky's voice had tightened into the narrow, focused register of a man verifying a catastrophe. "Stinkov's diagram is a sketch, a simplified skeleton, but the geometry is unmistakable. It describes a synthesis mode. It is a secondary stage of the transformation, a metabolic shift that bypasses the initial agitation of the early phases."

"What is the output?"

"The subject's biology begins producing the inhibitor's active compound directly. They have moved beyond the Rage Factor. They are cultivating the very thing Merck is currently scrambling to synthesize in a lab. The host becomes the laboratory, generating the resolution endogenously."

Jenna stood in a terrifying stillness. The centrifuge hummed its rhythmic, metallic prayer. Inside the containment vessel, the Gator Hole samples moved with a colonial, dreaming grace. She thought of Tanaka in Hokkaido—a woman maintained like a rare orchid, kept in a state of permanent, productive expiration. Maintenance was a euphemism for the slow harvest of a living cure.

"The Rage Factor is merely the byproduct, the smoke from the fire," Jenna said. Her voice felt like it was arriving from a great distance, a complete and terrible architecture. "They are farming the resolution. First, they manufacture the hunger, then they keep the survivors breathing just long enough to extract the feast. We are the factory. We are the quality-control. We are the feedstock."

"And the advertisement," Ricky added. "The Red Bee serves as the visible threat, the rogue ghost that makes the public scream for the medicine."

"Yes." She didn't need the end of his thought. The horror was already a closed loop.

She sat at her station and opened the synthesis model. She fed the new pathway from Stinkov's diagram into the simulation, mapping the imprecise lines against her own volatile blood work. The question pulsed in her marrow: was this synthesis a natural decay, or could it be provoked? If she could force the shift, if she could trigger the production of the inhibitor on her own terms, she could bypass the corporate timeline entirely.

"Ricky," she said.

"Yes."

"Do not tell me this is impossible. I am still forming the question."

"I'm listening."

"The expression on your face is already mourning the laws of physics." She began running the first simulation, her fingers dancing over the keys with a frantic, hexagonal grace. "If I can initiate this mode deliberately—if I can find a trigger that doesn't require me to burn through my remaining years to reach it—we can produce the inhibitor here. From me. We can flood the streets with the cure before the lawyers can even draft the injunctions."

The silence stretched, long and thin.

"That isn't impossible," Ricky said, his voice revising the boundaries of his world in real-time. "It is merely fatal. The metabolic load would likely shatter the organs before the first dose is even stable. But it is not impossible."

"Then model the wreckage. Find the threshold."

She heard his keyboard begin its staccato rhythm. Outside, the Superior City afternoon surrendered to a golden, horizontal light. The clouds shifted into their early-evening formation, a bruised gray that felt like a bruise on the sky. She had lived here for nine years, and the city still managed to surprise her with these moments of accidental, mythic beauty—the world offering a grace it did not owe.

He arrived at the loading dock at eight-fifteen, a presence felt through the acoustics of the industrial space.

Jenna heard the hesitation in his step before she saw him. He moved with the specific, clumsy noise of a man trying to be silent while his pulse screamed. She set down her pipette, cut the fume hood's exhaust, and stood at the threshold of the lab.

He looked to be twenty-five. The compound eyes processed him in a sudden rush of chemical data: a graduate student, three days into a sleepless descent, his blood a cocktail of elevated cortisol and adrenaline. He smelled of the specific, sharp ozone of someone watching their own sanity dissolve into a pattern they can no longer explain.

"The entomology department," he said, his voice trembling. "I saw the light beneath the door."

"You aren't one of mine."

"Engineering. Civil." He stood at the edge of the loading dock, hovering at the threshold with a terrified, structural courtesy. "I've been... I don't know how to speak it. The last two weeks have been a fever. I searched for 'unusual insect behavior' and the search led me here." He stopped, his hands shaking as he held up a glass jar. Inside, a honeybee sat, its wings vibrant and unnervingly calm. "This has been my shadow for three days. Every time I step into the sun, it finds me. Different bees, perhaps, but the same intent. They land. They wait. I am not afraid, but the weight of their attention is becoming a burden."

"Come inside," Jenna said.

His name was Dominic. He was a builder of bridges, a man who understood how loads were distributed and how structures failed under pressure. Now, the load-bearing beams of his own biology were warping. He hadn't been to Florida; he was a victim of a secondary deployment. Jenna ran the list of his haunts and found the breach in a shared study hall, a space recently 'renovated' by a contractor she recognized from the Palladian ledger. The rot was local now. It was in the vents. It was in the walls.

“The HVAC,” she said, her voice a low, resonant frequency that seemed to vibrate in the sterile air of the loading dock. “The compound is a mist, a ghost in the ventilation. It’s aerosolized, settling into the lungs of forty or fifty people in your building before they even realize the air has changed flavor.”

Dominic looked at the bee in the jar. It tapped the glass with a patient, rhythmic insistence, investigating the boundary of its world. “Is this a death sentence?”

“No.” She said it with the unwavering weight of a woman who had already mapped the terrain of the grave and found it wanting. “You don't carry the ancestral code that makes the transformation a flash-fire. For you, it’s a slower erosion—the compound is just turning up the volume on your soul, making the world feel louder, heavier, more urgent. It wants your pulse to race. It wants the high-frequency exhaust of your engagement.”

“The anger,” he whispered, the realization visible in the tightening of his jaw. “The last two weeks... I’ve been a stranger to my own temper. I’ve screamed at screens and fought ghosts in the comments.”

“That is the harvest,” Jenna said. She watched him, seeing the civil engineer's mind trying to find the load-bearing failure in his own biology. "The platforms you inhabit are tuned to the same frequencies as the compound's replication. When you engage, you aren't just scrolling; you're feeding the fire. For the next two weeks, you must choose the silence of the analog. Disconnect the copper. Burn the bridge to the digital void."

She handed him the management protocol, a document she had forged that afternoon with the surgical precision of a woman who knew the exact cost of a heartbeat. "Follow the grammar of this paper. Come back in four days. I'm building a resolution, and you are the first pillar."

Dominic took the paper as if it were a holy relic. "You know what this thing is," he said, a statement rather than a question.

"I am inhabiting it," she replied. "That is a much more useful form of knowledge."

He left, his footsteps echoing like a fading pulse across the concrete. Jenna stood in the doorway, the Superior City night pressing against her. The air tasted of wet pavement and the electric ghost of a million lives lived behind glass. She thought of Webb's assessment: You are angry about the right things.

She thought of the bee Dominic had left behind. It had been a mirror for his turbulence—calm when he was steady, frantic when he was frayed. A bond born of affinity, a molecular truth that like calls to like.

She stepped back into the lab, closing the door on the world. She didn't feel like a hero, or a victim, or even the Red Bee. She felt like the woman who had once written a dissertation on how love is a biological imperative, a transformative force that rewrites the DNA of the devoted. She had been right, and her truth had been stolen and weaponized.

She opened her spiral-bound notebook—the one with the coffee rings and the history of her own failures. She began to draw the synthesis protocol, her pen moving with a cold, rhythmic certainty. She didn't rush. Rushing was for the fearful, and fear was the product she was no longer willing to manufacture.

The bee sat in its jar, watching her with a compound gaze that felt like a quiet recognition.

Jenna reached out and twisted the lid.

The insect took flight in a soft, golden arc, landing on the back of her hand. It didn't sting; it simply sat there, a tiny weight of shared history.

“I know,” she whispered to the creature.

She returned to the work, the synthesis blooming on the page in a language of enzymes and intent. Outside, the city’s orange streetlights fought the encroaching dark. In a silent room in Bethesda, an old man waited with a file that had been a twenty-year burden, listening for the sound of an approaching storm.

Jenna Raleigh was the storm. She was going to Bethesda. And she was bringing the sting.

Chapter Four: The Rage

The notification arrived at 2:47 PM, puncturing the low hum of the lab while Jenna watched the centrifuge spin the red out of her history.

Her phone lay face-down on the stainless steel bench, its screen a hidden glow against the metal. The vibration was a distinct pulse—three short bursts, a heavy pause, one long thrum. It was a rhythmic binary she and Kayla had forged in 2019, a year defined by Jenna's optimistic attempt to build a language that survived her own absence. She had always lacked a talent for the immediate present. Her life was an accumulation of evidence, a patient harvest of proof that left a record even when she was elsewhere.

She ignored the first cycle. The centrifuge demanded her focus as it separated her blood into nameless layers. Her plasma was being rewritten. The pheromone was a silent engineer, assembling its framework through her lymphatic system with the cold persistence of a construction project rather than an infection. She watched the glass vials blur and thought of the synthesis pathway Ricky was mapping. Her body was deciding whether to become a savior or a refined biological resource for the highest bidder.

Three short. Pause. One long.

The rhythm repeated instantly, a frantic stutter that broke their established protocol. Kayla didn't break protocol.

Jenna gripped the phone. A screenshot sat in the notifications, forwarded from a ghost account. It was timestamped 3:17 AM—her own handle, the username she had used since 2011 to track entomology journals and log field data. The syntax was a perfect mimicry of her professional voice, but the content was a desecration.

The Freedom Fighters were government propaganda. Richard Raleigh was a useful idiot. Real resistance to tyranny doesn't wear a costume and take orders from Uncle Sam.

Kayla's message followed: *mom are you okay you posted some crazy shit.*

Jenna stared at the glowing glass. She remembered 3:17 AM with the surgical clarity the pheromone provided in place of sleep. She had been at this bench, cross-referencing Stinkov's diagrams against her own blood-work, lost in the focused patience she had inherited from Richard's meticulously kept case files. She had never touched the screen.

She opened the platform. Nineteen posts had been vomited into her feed between 3:00 and 5:30 AM. They carried the precise compression of her academic writing, layered with the distinct texture of contempt she had cultivated over two decades of watching her funding wither and her dissertation vanish into the vaults of NIH review boards. The pheromone had mapped her grievances and found their most effective outlet.

The NIH buries research that threatens pharmaceutical revenue. I have direct evidence. The people protecting the system are not defending science; they are defending profit margins.

Colony collapse disorder is a symptom, not a cause. The cause is deliberate. The people who know this are being managed.

My great-uncle died so that the thing he was fighting could incorporate and buy a senator. I have spent twenty years being careful about saying this. I am done being careful.

She read them three times. The rhythm was her own. The rage belonged to her—the accumulation of every professional door slammed with a polite, bureaucratic smile since 2009. The pheromone had harvested her soul and expressed it in a form designed to destroy her credibility while remaining hauntingly accurate.

A pinned reply on the most inflammatory post contained a fragment of the Sweetwater Holdings incorporation documents. It was a tease, a revelation meant to incite engagement without providing the leverage of proof. It made her look like a woman in the throes of a psychotic break rather than a whistleblower.

Stinkov was the architect. He had studied her the way she studied a hive—her patterns, her productive peaks, the vocabulary of her grief. He had constructed these digital shadows to compromise her before she could move, proving to his subscribers that the pheromone could be used to override the personhood of the host. She was a biological advertisement for her own obsolescence.

She dialed Kayla. Voicemail. She called again, the harmonics in her throat vibrating in time with the lab's fluorescent hum. On the third attempt, Kayla answered. Her voice was thin, distant, a sound filtered through tears she refused to acknowledge as a vulnerability.

"Mom."

"I didn't post those." Jenna’s words surged, the pheromone pushing her to justify, to feed the cycle of engagement. "Kayla, I was in the lab. I was working. The things they said—they aren't entirely false, but I didn't write them. I was hacked."

"They sound like you." Kayla’s voice was flat, a diagnostic tone that cut deeper than anger. "Not the part about great-great-uncle Richard. I know you don't think he was an idiot. But the rest. The way you talk about the department. The way you talked about Dad when he left." A pause, the sound of a daughter measuring the wreckage of a mother. "The way you’ve always talked about saving people. Like the world owed you the opportunity to be a hero, and you were just mad it kept refusing you."

Jenna went silent. The centrifuge finished its cycle with a decisive, mechanical click. The lab was suddenly still, save for the low roar of the exhaust hood and the muffled, indifferent thrum of Superior City outside the cinderblock walls.

"I have to go," Jenna whispered.

"You always have to go," Kayla replied, and the line went dead.

Jenna looked at the centrifuge. The blood had separated. The layers were clear, distinct, and utterly alien. She had six months to live, a daughter who saw through her like a window, and a ghost in her machine who was currently using her legacy to set the world on fire.

"That's not fair," she said. She knew the word was a ghost. Fairness belonged to the era before her marrow became a patent.

"I know," Kayla replied. Her voice possessed the heavy vibration of a stone settling in deep water. "I know it's not fair. But it's what I see. And whatever is happening to you—" She stopped. Jenna heard the sharp inhalation of a child standing at the edge of an abyss, choosing between the safety of a lie and the jagged edge of the truth. "I looked up Hymenoptera. You left your laptop open when you visited last month. I was looking for your heating pad, for my cramps, and I saw the files. The images of your eyes. The names."

The cold thread in Jenna's chest spasmed, a needle-thin ice-storm in her veins. "Kayla—"

"Chen. Okafor. Tanaka." Her daughter recited the litany of the harvested with a flat precision that tasted of cold iron. "I know what the file says about timelines. I’ve done the math. I’ve been living in that equation for three weeks."

Jenna was already in motion. She shed the lab coat like a dead skin, her fingers fumbling for the keys. A primal drive surged within her, a desperate need to bridge the distance, but a cold realization arrested her movement. The pheromone had identified Kayla as the ultimate catalyst. Her daughter was the highest-yield engagement, a biological snare woven from sixteen years of shared history. To go to her now was to surrender to the harvest. The system needed her driving, panicked and visible, a frantic organism providing the high-octane fuel of maternal terror.

She stood in the center of the lab and forced her heart to slow.

"I'm not coming," she said. The words felt like lead in her mouth. "Not right now. Not while I'm a vector."

A hollow silence followed. "Okay." Kayla's voice shifted, the fear giving way to a weary understanding. "Okay. Good."

"Close the platform, Kayla. Shut the world out. Those posts are bait, a rhythmic pulse designed to generate a response. Every reply and every shared fragment feeds the replication. They are farming our outrage." Jenna looked at her hands. The hexagonal bloom on her knuckles had become an ordinary detail, a warning of the new baseline. "Please. Just disappear for today."

"I closed it an hour ago," Kayla said. "I thought about texting you earlier. I didn't because I thought you needed to find the shore yourself. I thought if you saw the fire and ran to me, it would only burn us both."

"You were right."

"I know." A pause followed, one where Jenna could hear the heavy cost of a daughter becoming the parent. "Mom. The images in the file... you look like someone is changing the channel. You're the same station, but the signal is tuned to the void."

"That is exactly what it is," Jenna whispered.

"Then stay," Kayla said. "Stay in the lab. Finish the work. Don't come here because the chemical in your blood thinks it's a primal necessity. Come when it's your own idea."

Jenna ended the call. She stood in her storage-closet sanctuary and breathed, counting the seconds. She noted the pheromone's agitation at the interrupted sequence, a frustration that felt like a swarm of needles beneath her skin. When the sensation receded, it left a harder, crystalline clarity. The system's rage was undirected and visible, a performance for the cameras. Her own rage possessed a target.

She sat down and returned to the synthesis model. She became the work.

⁂

The truck arrived as a glitch in the world's order. Jenna would return to the data later, seeking an explanation for the anomaly, but in the moment, it was simply a collision of fates.

She had gone out at four to harvest atmospheric samples. It was a mundane task, a collection of particulates from the loading dock and the surrounding block required for Ricky's transmission models. She carried the array and a data tablet, her mind occupied by the synthesis protocol and the upcoming journey to Bethesda. She was not thinking of Stinkov or the engagement metrics climbing in the digital dark.

The vehicle cut through the crosswalk at Vance and 7th. It wasn't moving at a reckless speed, but it moved with the blind indifference of a machine without a pilot. Jenna and two other pedestrians were forced to halt as the metal mass completed the turn. The driver did not notice. He was a ghost haunting his own life, a marionette dancing to the pulse of a screen held in his lap.

The truck slowed for a red light thirty feet ahead, and the driver remained submerged in the false god of his device.

The ignition happened without her consent. The cold thread flared, a rhythmic vibration of the void. Her production rate spiked, a surge of power that flooded her throat and vocal range with a harmonic distortion. Her vision sharpened, the world fracturing into a thousand points of hyper-focus.

She was at the truck's window before the thought had fully formed. Her left hand held the collection array; her right was a braced weight against the door. Through the metal, she felt the thermal signature of the man inside, a warm animal lost in a digital mirror.

"Hey." The word arrived in layers, a buzzing vibration that rattled the glass. The driver looked up, his face a mask of startled blankness. His screen showed a forum thread from Stinkov's board, a digital hive Jenna recognized instantly.

"The light is green," she said. It had been green for four seconds. "And there were people in that crosswalk."

The man stared at her. Jenna watched the fear take root as he processed her eyes—the bruised red of the sclera, the needle-narrow pupils. It was a terrifying recognition. He reached for his phone, the modern reflex for a threat he couldn't understand.

"Put it down." The harmonic in her voice sharpened. The truck's electrical display flickered and stuttered in sympathy with her frequency. The driver's hand dropped as if his muscles had forgotten their purpose. "Just drive. The light is green."

He drove. Jenna stood at the intersection and watched him vanish into the gray afternoon. She held the collection array in a trembling hand, her pulse a rhythmic thud that refused to subside. She had made a choice she would not have made a week ago. She had performed for the cameras she knew were watching from every corner. She had stepped into the intersection and fed the beast, and the beast was already beginning to howl for more.

The word arrived in layers, a choral distortion that felt less like speech and more like an environmental pressure. Through the glass, she watched the driver—mid-thirties, his features slack in the blue-light glow of one of Stinkov's boards—look up with the startled, hollow blankness of a man interrupted in a deeply private ritual.

"The light is green," she said. It had been green for four seconds, a lifetime in the rhythmic timing of the city. "And there were people in that crosswalk."

He stared. She watched the gears of his perception grind as they caught on the wrongness of her eyes. Even behind the pharmaceutical-grade contacts, the geometry was an affront to the human baseline. Fear sparked in his marrow, producing the modern reflex: the phone rising like a shield or a prayer to record the anomaly.

"Put it down." The harmonics sharpened, a visceral rasp that vibrated in the truck's chassis. The dashboard display flickered, a momentary stutter in the vehicle's electronic heartbeat, and the driver's hand dropped. It was not a choice; it was a biological surrender, the muscles forgetting the intention of the reach. "Just drive. The light is green."

He drove. She stood at the jagged edge of the intersection and watched him vanish into the gray afternoon, the collection array heavy in her left hand. The pheromone began its slow, tidal subsidence, a withdrawal of power that left the air tasting of ozone and spent adrenaline. Superior City moved around her with the exhausted indifference of a place that had long ago traded its sense of wonder for a sense of survival.

A phone had been recording. The compound eyes had mapped the angle from the far corner before she had even crossed the asphalt—the specific, held-breath stillness of a witness capturing a ghost. She had known the camera was there and she had stepped into the frame anyway. The math she had done at the production peak was a treacherous arithmetic, a logic optimized for visibility while wearing the stolen face of a reasonable response.

She gathered the atmospheric samples and retreated to the loading dock.

⁂

Ricky's text arrived at 5:48 PM: *It's on the platform. You're trending. Someone cross-referenced the footage with the account posts and called it a breakdown. I'm sorry.*

She read it twice, the red in her iris pulsing in the dim lab light. She texted back: *Model's ready. Come in.*

He appeared at six, bearing coffee and the heavy silence of a man who had rehearsed a eulogy he wasn't ready to deliver. He sat across from her, his screen a bright wound in the shadows of the storage closet, reflecting trend data she already felt in the static of her skin.

"It isn't a breakdown," she said.

"I know."

"It's a choreography. Stinkov had enough of my syntax to ghost-write the posts, and Sweetwater has enough structural reach into the platform to ensure the initial bloom of engagement." She had spent the last two hours translating her shock into documentation, anchoring the chaos in the cold safety of a ledger. "The footage is the anchor. I made a choice today that required the compound's interference to execute. That is the only part of the record that is accurate."

"The choice was to tell a man to look at the road," Ricky said, his voice straining for a normalcy that no longer existed.

"The choice was to use a weaponized frequency to compel a human being in a public square. The outcome was a courtesy; the mechanism was an extraction." She met his gaze, her narrow pupils holding the light. "I am not performing accountability for an audience. I am mapping the threshold so I can find it again in the dark."

Ricky looked down at the phone. "It's been ringing. Dale. Four times. Then Kayla. Then a Maryland prefix."

Jenna took the burner. It wasn't the Bethesda number, but the geography was close enough to feel like a tether. She dialed.

The man on the other end spoke with the frictionless, cushioned authority of a lawyer. Dale had retained them. Evidence of a medical episode. Temporary guardianship. A recommendation for a voluntary evaluation. He used the word *voluntary* as if it were a mercy, though the subtext carried the cold weight of a cage.

"Which facility," she asked.

"The evaluation would be conducted at a BrinCell-certified behavioral health center," the lawyer said.

"Thank you." She ended the call and let the silence of the lab settle.

BrinCell-certified. Dale, with his reliable, catastrophic talent for accepting the wrong kind of help, was hand-delivering her to the processing plant. He would think he was protecting Kayla; he would think he was saving Jenna from her own unraveling. He treated corporate resources like atmospheric oxygen—ubiquitous, neutral, and necessary. It was the quality that had made him possible to love once, and impossible to remain bound to.

"He doesn't understand," she said, her voice a low vibration. "He thinks he's building a sanctuary."

"Does it matter?" Ricky asked.

"Not for the work. No." She looked at the synthesis model, the forty-eight hours of sweat and shadowed biology that had produced a protocol she couldn't yet prove. It was a bridge to Bethesda, to Webb, to the ghost of Tanaka. "I need you to move tonight, before the containment arrives."

"They're coming tonight?"

"The footage is six hours old. The narrative is set. They won't wait for the morning." She pulled up the encrypted file, a digital heartbeat of her own defiance. "Take the protocol. Take the genealogy and the evidence of the compromise. Get them off the university servers. Find a place where Palladian's shadow doesn't reach."

"The university cloud is—"

"Funded by Meridian. Which is Palladian. Which is the hunt." She watched him absorb the reach of the machine. "Use your own hardware. Use a key only you know. I don't want the password. If they compel you, I want the choice to be yours alone. I want the decision to belong to a human being, not a subject."

He remained silent, the practical intelligence that had first drawn her to him now manifesting as a grim, focused industriousness. He moved with the rhythm of someone who understood that survival was a series of small, accurate movements.

"You are shielding me," he said, the words heavy with an unwanted debt.

"I am distributing the risk according to the terrain," Jenna replied, watching the progress bars crawl across the screen. "One of us has to be the ghost. The other has to be the distraction. That is the only math that preserves the work."

"And if they come for the lab?"

"You speak the truth. You are an assistant. You followed the curriculum. You saw me leave, and I seemed... coherent." She paused, the second harmonic in her voice buzzing like a wire in a gale. "The reality of where I go after this is a burden I refuse to place on your ledger. Do not look for me."

"Where is the destination, Jenna?"

She touched the burner phone in her drawer, feeling the cold, plastic certainty of it. BEEKEEPER. A basement lined with lead and old paper, miles from the reach of the digital hive. "A place where the ink stays on the page and the signals die in the air. Three days. Tonight, I play the part of the ex-wife in crisis. Tonight, I go to Dale."

⁂

The BrinCell extraction team arrived with the quiet, terrifying efficiency of a surgical strike. Three vehicles, dark and featureless, rolled into the loading dock at 9:23 PM. They were private security—the kind of men who wore tactical gear with the casual grace of athletic wear. Dale had been meticulous; involving the police would have generated a public record, an invitation for inquiry that neither he nor his corporate masters desired. They offered her a practiced, professional warmth, the kind of sympathy used by veterinarians before the needle. It was a suffocating kindness, difficult to resist because it mimicked the shape of genuine care.

Jenna went without a struggle. She carried the hard-shell case as if it were a holy relic, refusing to let the team lead touch the latches. He measured the weight of her gaze, the bruised red of her eyes behind the contacts, and calculated the cost of a confrontation. He decided the case could wait.

The evaluation center sat on the metropolitan fringe, a glass-and-steel monolith renovated into a sanctuary of clinical shadows. The interior was a masterpiece of soft edges and indirect lighting, a space designed to bleed the fight out of a subject. Jenna sat in a room that smelled of ozone and lavender, facing two clinicians who spoke in the measured tones of people accustomed to managing gods.

"Have you experienced changes in your sensory threshold?" the first one asked, her stylus hovering over a tablet.

"Yes," Jenna said.

"Changes in the duration or intensity of emotional cycles?"

"Yes."

"Any behavior you would categorize as uncharacteristic? A loss of impulse regulation?"

"Once. Today. I have been documenting the interference pattern."

"A heightened sense of purpose? A clarity regarding your objectives?"

"Yes."

"Would you describe this clarity as distressing?"

Jenna leaned forward. "No."

The second clinician hesitated, her hand performing a subtle, jagged notation on the screen. Jenna watched the movement through the fractured lens of her compound vision, reading the hesitation in the pixels, the way the light refracted off the glass. She had missed the expected mark. The *Hymenoptera* file demanded a subject in distress, an organism producing the high-yield pheromones of fear and confusion. Jenna's response was a deviation, an anomaly in the harvest.

They classified her as *responsive to observation*. It was a terminal designation, a shelf where they kept the specimens they couldn't yet control.

At 11:00 PM, they surrendered her to Dale's custody. He took her to his "glass rectangle," a monument to his own persistent vanity perched over the Columbia River. They fastened an ankle monitor to her—a heavy, biometric shackle that broadcasted her heartrate, her location, and the chemical composition of her sweat to a server in Delaware. The team lead gave the orientation with the boredom of a prison guard. Permitted zones. Flagged perimeters. The protocol for the extraction of a resource.

"The garage," Jenna said, her voice a low, vibrating rasp. "My gear is in the case."

"The case stays in the garage. That is a flagged zone. You may request access in writing."

"Thank you."

⁂

The house at midnight was a tomb of expensive transparency. It smelled of lemon wax and the sterile breath of the climate control—a temperature set to preserve the furniture rather than comfort the inhabitant. Dale was still in Florida, leaving Jenna alone in a cage of his own design. She moved through the lower floor, the compound eyes reading the electromagnetic ghosts of the room. The listening devices in the kitchen speakers sang in a frequency of surveillance. The camera in the smoke detector watched with an unblinking, digital eye.

She stood in the hallway at 12:15 AM, mapping the mesh of sensors. The garage door was a barrier of infrared and motion triggers, but the system had a blind spot. A gap in the alignment of the perimeter and the garage threshold.

Fourteen inches.

The suit was on a shelf between a pressure washer and a rack of unused road bikes. The monitor on her ankle would scream if she crossed the line. She noted the distance, the exact pulse of the security node, and the silence of the river below. She did not reach for the door. She memorized the failure in the design and walked upstairs.

In the guest bathroom, steam rose to choke the obsidian mirror as she held her wrists under a scalding flow. The faucet was a heavy, silver-tongued thing Dale had chosen with the same hunger he applied to every acquisition after the divorce—a frantic attempt to fill a hollow center with expensive metal. The heat bit into her skin, grounding her. She thought of Kayla, who had carried the names of three dead women in her mind for weeks, conducting the grim arithmetic of her mother's mortality in silence. Her daughter had watched the clock of Jenna's biology wind down and waited for Jenna to find the key herself.

The pheromone withdrew, its evening peak subsiding into a low, rhythmic thrum. It was a receding tide, pulling back from the shoreline of her nerves only to gather strength for the next surge. The evaluation, the monitoring, the arrival at this transparent prison—all of it had been processed through that alien frequency. Now, in the hollow of the night, the silence felt heavy, a precursor to a tectonic shift in her blood.

She dried her hands. The towel felt like sandpaper. She sat on the edge of the tub, her spine curved against the porcelain.

The burner phone rested in the interior pocket of her blazer, hanging on the guest room door. She had moved it from the lab drawer with the fluid motion of a magician, a small act of defiance the monitor couldn't register. The shackle on her ankle tracked her pulse and her proximity to the kitchen, but it couldn't read the weight of the plastic in her pocket.

Two days remained. Forty-eight hours in a glass cage, producing the harvest they expected while she wove a different shroud. She had the synthesis protocol on Ricky's hardware. She had Webb's number waiting in the dark. She had the fourteen-inch gap near the garage threshold—a sliver of freedom just out of reach.

The clinicians at the evaluation center had labeled her "responsive to observation." In the Hymenoptera ledger, this was the mark of the anomaly. "Responsive to treatment" was the goal; it meant the subject had surrendered to the amplification, their soul consumed to fuel the production cycle. She was the outlier described in the file's cold footnotes. She was the one who looked into the throat of the machine and studied the mechanics of the gears instead of screaming at the teeth.

They would adjust. The resource was non-standard, which made her dangerous. But the resource also possessed a map they didn't know she had.

She thought of Tanaka, held in a facility in Hokkaido. The "subject maintenance" payments were a confession written in ink. Tanaka was a harvest that never ended, a living template kept in a state of permanent, productive expiration. Jenna saw the framework of the machine now, the way it bled the extraordinary until there was nothing left but a natural cause.

If the synthesis mode could be provoked rather than suffered—if she could seize the timeline and force the bloom on her own terms—the machine would choke on the result. Tanaka had been a victim of the process. Jenna intended to be the architect of its collapse.

The monitor emitted a sharp, clinical beep. She had drifted toward the hallway, her mind mapping the darkness. The kitchen lay ahead, a flagged zone of hard edges and knives. She stepped back, retreating two paces until the warning subsided.

She was a specimen in a jar. She was producing the black water they craved. But beneath the chemical fog, she was planning. She refused to give them the rage they had designed her to feel. Fury was a feedstock; clarity was a weapon.

She returned to the sink and ran the water again, hotter this time. She watched the hexagonal patterns on her knuckles, the skin healing with a speed that felt like a betrayal. She thought of Dominic, the boy with the bee in the jar. He had seen the wrongness in the world and offered it a safe harbor instead of a blow.

Her great-uncle had understood the truth that the Freedom Fighter archives had polished into myth. A hive's intelligence didn't live in the queen or the workers. It lived in the spaces between them, in the patient accumulation of small, accurately reported facts. It was a collective capacity built of care.

Richard hadn't been a soldier. He had been a beekeeper who learned that the only way to survive the swarm was to become a part of its rhythm. Jenna gripped the edge of the sink, the heat of the water turning her skin a bruised red, and prepared to find that rhythm in the dark.

To dismantle a colony, one does not assault the workers. One alters the environment until the old ways of being become impossible. This was the beekeeper's truth, a lesson written in the marrow of her lineage.

She dried her hands, the skin feeling tight and foreign. In the guest room, she reached for the blazer draped over the door's hook like a shed skin. Her fingers found the burner phone in the interior pocket. It was a cold, plastic heart, heavy with the weight of potential. She held it for a long minute, tracing the single contact programmed under BEEKEEPER.

Webb was a ghost on the other end of a two-day horizon. She resisted the urge to dial. The house was a glass trap, a crystalline lung that breathed through microphones hidden in the kitchen speakers and unblinking eyes nested within the smoke detectors. To speak now would be to scream into the teeth of the machine. She let the silence of the room settle over her, understanding that the line to Webb was a secret well-kept, a path through the woods that the system had not yet paved over. Two days of performance was a small tax to pay when the alternative was a predictable failure.

She returned the device to its hiding place and surrendered herself to Dale's guest bed. The mattress offered the sterile comfort of a showroom floor. On her ankle, the monitor hummed, a parasite feeding on her vitals. It translated her pulse and the strange, metallic heat of her blood into a digital ledger for men who mistook her for a commodity. They saw a resource, a high-yield crop to be harvested and bottled. They saw the byproduct of a great-uncle's devotion and called it a patent.

She allowed them the illusion of control. For forty-eight hours, she would play the part of the feedstock.

Sleep remained an elective she could no longer afford. The pheromone had replaced the need for rest with a humming, electric readiness that vibrated in the base of her skull. She lay perfectly still in the dark, her mind a loom weaving the threads of the synthesis protocol. She mapped the fourteen-inch gap by the garage, a sliver of darkness where the sensors went blind. She thought of the letter to Webb and the woman in Hokkaido. Tanaka was a mirror held up in a distant room, a fragment of herself waiting for a reconciliation that Jenna intended to provide.

Below the glass house, the Columbia River moved with the heavy, unhurried indifference of deep time. It flowed past the foundations, carrying the mountain's cold into the sea, oblivious to the surveillance and the chemical revolutions occurring above its surface. Jenna waited in that same current. She inhabited the stillness Richard had mastered between deployments—the focused, predatory patience of an organism that knows the storm is coming and has already decided to become the wind. She remained precisely, unmistakably herself, a red sting held in reserve until the world turned and the conditions finally changed.

Chapter Five: Beekeeping

The basalt cliffs of the Columbia held the transparent cage as if it were a rare insect pinned to the gorge. Three sides of the house offered the illusion of absolute sight, while the fourth—a slab of grey concrete—stood as a monument to the unobserved. Dale had found the design in a glossy spread and worshipped its futility; in a home made of light, he believed the shadow was the true revelation. He possessed a talent for reading symbols into everything except the rot in their bed.

Jenna's world had shrunk to the upper floor. The stairs weren't barred by steel, only by the shrill electronic pulse of the shackle. It sang a warning whenever she drifted toward the kitchen—a landscape of ceramic edges and blades. It wailed near the garage, where the hard case lay dormant between a dusty pressure washer and the skeletal remains of road bikes Dale had never ridden. Even through the floorboards, she inhaled the suit. It wasn't the scent of polymer or metal; it was a pheromonal siren call. Her biology recognized the armor as a long-lost limb, a prosthetic of the soul finally coming home.

Dale's voice arrived from Florida, thin and tinny through the phone. He spoke of wellbeing and stability, a liturgy of concern meant to mask the sacrifice he'd made. Jenna listened to the pauses, catching the sulfurous rot of his lies. It wasn't a total fabrication, but something more precise—the chemical stench of a man who has convinced himself that a betrayal is actually a mercy. He believed he was shielding their daughter, Kayla. He simply refused to see the price tag attached to the shield.

She offered him the expected platitudes and hung up. Staring at the river's indifferent flow, she ran the calculations. The protocol lived in her marrow now, a sequence hidden from the house's electronic eyes. She had sent the hard copies with Ricky; now she only had the rhythm of the work pulsing in her skull.

Rosa arrived at eight. She was fifty-three, with children at the university and in the Navy, and she was clean. Jenna had mapped the woman's scent on the first morning—no traces of BrinCell's oily fingerprints. Rosa moved through the glass cage with the weary grace of a woman who knew that a house was just a machine that needed cleaning. Yet, the walls listened. A microphone nested in the kitchen; a camera watched from the smoke detector. Jenna played the role of the quiet invalid, requesting tea with the courtesy of a condemned queen. Hunger clawed at her, but not for Rosa's pantry staples. Her metabolism had shifted, craving the dense proteins needed to fuel the fire in her veins. When the house was empty, she stood at the window, consuming raw fuel with the cold efficiency of a predator. She was becoming lean, efficient, and dangerous.

On the third day, a box arrived. "Bloom & Settle," the label read, marked with a honeybee of a red-gold hue that had never graced a commercial palette. Jenna waited for Rosa to retreat upstairs before descending. The monitor shrieked, a digital fever rising as she breached the kitchen, but she snatched the package before the alert could trigger a lockdown.

In the windowless guest bathroom, she worked beneath the roar of the ventilation fan. The bath salts and tea were the skin of the gift; the meat lay beneath. A vintage dryer that held no heat. A yoga mat that unrolled into a frame. Ricky had understood the unspoken need.

She pieced the suit together in the dark, her fingers moving by the memory of the itch in her blood. The microfiber joints locked with a hiss of pressurized seals. After eight years, the exoskeleton didn't just fit; it evolved. It mapped the rewritten geography of her frame. The helmet sealed, and the HUD flared to life, a red dawn in her eyes.

Diagnostics ran for forty seconds—a lifetime for a system that usually knew its master instantly. It flagged the anomalies in bone density, the hexagonal lattice reinforcing her knuckles, and the neural conductivity surging like a storm through her nerves. Pheromone levels sat at a baseline four hundred percent above the old human records. She wasn't wearing the suit anymore. They were becoming a single, terrifying intent.

The infirmity was an illusion; the truth was industrial. Jenna watched the HUD carve the air into data points, dissecting the protein chains she had dragged from the mire of Gator Hole. The machine didn't care about her comfort, only the yield. It cross-referenced her pulse with the alien blueprint, returning a cold verdict in the stark language of the inevitable:

SYNTHESIS PATHWAY ACTIVITY: DETECTED. STAGE: TRANSITIONAL. FULL EXPRESSION: 9–14 DAYS.

She read the numbers until they burned into her retinas. This was the ghost in Stinkov's machine, the hidden chapter omitted from the patents. Her body was no longer just a host for an infection; it was an organic forge, beginning to hammer out its own antidote. The process was embryonic, a biological scaffolding rising cell by cell. BrinCell had likely envisioned her as a specimen in a jar, never anticipating that the specimen would begin to rewrite the jar's composition.

A slow exhale fogged the visor. The HUD logged the shift in her breath, a minute fluctuation in the vacuum of her focus. On her ankle, the heavy biometric shackle remained silent, blinded by the suit's shielding. Ricky's foresight felt like a heavy debt; he had anticipated the electronic cage before she had even stepped into it.

The air in the house grew thick with newfound meaning. She tasted the sulfurous rot of the listening devices transmitting from the kitchen. She sensed the clean, unburdened honesty of Rosa's scent drifting from the hallway above. Even the river below the floorboards had a voice now—a deep, tectonic groan resonating through the structural steel. She was evolving past the limits of her skin, an apex predator emerging from the husk of a researcher.

At eleven AM, she reached out through the blood. The communication wasn't a radio wave but a vibration in the marrow, a frequency she had discovered in the dark. It bypassed the silicon world entirely, traveling through the living tissue of the house.

"The package arrived," Ricky's voice crackled in her mind. It lacked the hesitation of their earlier days. "I trust the yoga mat met your standards."

"A masterpiece of misdirection," Jenna replied. She could hear the rhythmic creak of his chair, a relic of a university that had long since stopped investing in anything but its own ego. "I've run the diagnostics. The synthesis is transitional."

"It's accelerating," Ricky said, his tone sharpening. "My models gave you weeks. The suit says days. We're losing the luxury of patience. I've secured the Merck prototype—the blocker. A contact in their clinical trials reached out. He's seen the shadow of the hawk; he's been exposed to the aerosolized strain in their vents. He's terrified enough to be useful."

"I need that prototype, Ricky. Not to stop the change, but to map the resistance. If the blocker chokes the late-stage production, I need to feel where the gears bind before I force the timeline."

"You're going to use yourself as a titration curve," Ricky said. There was no judgment in his voice, only the flat acknowledgment of a necessity. "Stinkov has gone loud. He's stopped lurking in the fringes and moved into the light. He's rebranded the contagion as 'neurochemical liberty.' Four thousand disciples are paying for the privilege of their own unraveling. He's selling rage as a nootropic, a supplement for the modern soul."

Jenna watched a spider navigate the corner of the ceiling, its movements a sequence of predatory math. "He’s become a useful monster. BrinCell needs a villain to justify the chains they’re preparing to sell as a cure. He’s the storm that makes people beg for the shelter of their labs."

"He believes he’s the architect," Ricky said. "He thinks he’s the one holding the leash."

"He’s a component in a machine he hasn’t bothered to study," Jenna said. "He’s the noise that masks the signal. But does he see the horizon? Does he know the biology is about to render his patents obsolete?"

"Stinkov's diagrams are the sketches of a man looking at a map through a keyhole," Ricky said, his voice thinning across the encrypted line. "He recognizes the surge, the peak where the subject becomes something more, but he’s anchored to the idea of a crash. He believes the system has to fail, that the host is just a fuse meant to blow. He hasn't seen anyone breathe through the heat without a cage to hold them."

"Because no one has ever been given the chance to walk," Jenna replied. She held her hands up, watching the light catch the suit’s gauntlets. Beneath the plating, her knuckles looked like a fossilized honeycomb, a rigid design rising from the meat of her palms. The suit didn't just house her anymore; it translated the silent conversation of her cells into a language of steel and light. "The Hokkaido site. Give me the rest."

"I’m chasing ghosts through four different shell companies," Ricky said. The sound of keys clicking—a frantic, rhythmic tapping—became the background of her thoughts. "The ledger is a maze, but the energy draw is a heartbeat. This facility is sucking down power at a rate that only makes sense for biological deep-freeze. And the checks haven't stopped. Thirty-one months of maintenance payments. Continuous."

"Thirty-one months." Jenna tasted the copper of her own tongue. Tanaka's death certificate was a two-year-old lie, a piece of paper meant to bury a resource that was still breathing. "She's alive. They kept her heart beating two months past her funeral."

"If we're looking at the same woman, Jenna. It's a massive leap."

"It's her." The certainty didn't come from a screen; it arrived through the shifting pressure in her chest. The pheromone provided a colonial intuition, a heavy, unasked-for awareness that connected her to the missing woman. Like calls to like. "She hit the transition. She started producing. They couldn't let that kind of yield go to waste, so they built a vault around her. Thirty-one months of being a human tap, Ricky. Think about the rot of that."

"I am," he whispered.

"Bethesda is the only way through. Webb's archive is the map for the vault's lungs. He'll have the entry codes and the internal blueprints that corporate law has scrubled from the web." She checked the HUD. The suit was hungry, its power cells trickling down. "The blocker. Can you bridge the distance?"

"Two days," Ricky promised. "That's the window."

The package arrived on the fifth day, nestled in a crate of raw Willamette Valley honey. The irony wasn't lost on her—the sticky, amber sweetness cloaking a chemical shackle. She dragged the jar into the guest bathroom and locked the door, the ventilation fan roaring above her like a dying engine.

She ran a quick titration. The formulation was slick, a parasite molecule designed to seize the receptors before the hive-code could settle. It was a lock meant for a door already hanging on its hinges. It wouldn't tear down the new structures, but it would freeze the carpenters mid-strike.

She swallowed the dose.

For four minutes, the world remained a vibrant, sensory assault. Then, the connection snapped.

The cold thread in her chest—the vibrating cord that connected her to the river, the house, and the unseen swarm—simply died. There was no slow fade, no gentle tapering of the signal. The silence was absolute. Jenna fell to the bathroom floor. It wasn't a failure of her muscles, but a sudden, violent reintroduction to the mundane weight of the planet.

The tile was cold. Truly, bitingly cold. For three weeks, she had processed temperature as a distant data point, a flicker on a HUD. Now, the chill bit into her skin with a cruel, forgotten intimacy. Her hands shook, the borrowed grace of the insectoid transition replaced by a primitive, human tremor.

The ache in her lower back arrived with the force of a debt collector. Her forty-two-year-old frame screamed at her. The compound had been masking the cost of her movements, papering over the tears in her muscles and the friction in her joints. It had turned her into a high-performance engine while ignoring the smoke rising from the valves. Without the chemical shielding, she was just a tired woman on a cold floor, broken by the sheer exertion of existing.

She lay there, a specimen of her own curiosity. The compound didn't just enhance; it hid the price. It allowed the host to burn until there was nothing left but ash, and then it withdrew the veil. No wonder they died of natural causes. The body just realized all at once that it was already dead.

She watched the clock on the HUD. Eleven minutes. The half-life of the blocker was a brief, agonizing window.

Slowly, the silence began to fray. The hum returned, but the texture had changed. It wasn't the jagged, frantic buzzing of the early days—the Rage that demanded a target. It was a low, structural thrum. The carpenters in her blood had gone back to work, but they were no longer building for a war. They were building for a permanent state.

Stinkov had called this stage transitional, a word that felt too soft for the structural overhaul of a nervous system. The early phases fed on the host's fire, using cortisol and adrenaline as a feedstock for the swarm. But this late stage—this was about survival. The biology was choosing stability. It didn't want her angry; it wanted her to last. It needed a vessel that wouldn't shatter under the weight of the crown.

She stood up, leaning against the sink as the chemical warmth flowed back into her limbs, masking the pain once more. She was a factory now, a living manufacture of something the patents couldn't name.

"Time to see Webb," she whispered to the mirror. Her pupils remained narrow, predatory slits, even as the human Jenna tried to find her way back to the surface.

The vertical ascent of her spine triggered a fresh cascade of data across the visor. The diagnostics flickered in a bruised violet hue. RESUMED. TRANSITIONAL. 8–13 DAYS.

The machine in her marrow had shaved twenty-four hours off the countdown. The blocker's retreat had left a vacuum, and her biology had rushed to fill the void with a tactical surge. Information, cold and absolute, was the only currency Jenna had ever trusted. She tucked the Merck prototype into the suit's medical bay with the reverence of a priestess handling a cursed relic. It offered no salvation, only a momentary pause in the rhythm of her transformation—a lock on a door that was already being kicked off its hinges.

Thursday arrived with a storm front bruising the Cascades. Jenna had paced the glass rectangle for days, dissecting her own longing. She weighed the desire to see Kayla against the baseline of the pheromone, searching for a parasitic spike that would signal her daughter was being used as emotional fuel. The signal remained flat, a tectonic stillness. The wanting was human. It was hers.

When the bell chimed, the house groaned in the wind. Jenna moved through the foyer, the transparent walls turning the afternoon into a stage of shifting greys. There was no sanctuary in this place, only the perpetual exposure of the cage.

Kayla stood at the threshold, a sixteen-year-old ghost of Jenna's former self. She was armored in a zipped jacket, her posture a fortress of observation. The compound eyes carved the girl into layers: the sharp ozone of anxiety, the floral scent of visceral affection, and beneath it all, a chemical signature that vibrated like a low-frequency hum.

"You look—" Kayla's voice caught on the jagged edges of her mother's new face.

"I know," Jenna said, stepping into the shadow. "Enter."

They sat on a couch designed for aesthetics rather than the comfort of human spines. The river churned below them, a grey muscle through the glass. Jenna watched the girl's pulse in her throat.

"You're pregnant," Jenna said.

Kayla didn't flinch. The news shifted the air, but the girl remained centered. "I intended to say that myself."

"I am sorry the timing converged with the Hymenoptera file," Jenna offered.

"Are you?" Kayla's gaze was a scalpel. "Or is the hive-mind offering its condolences?"

"It is me," Jenna replied, anchoring her voice to the cold tile of the floor. "I have spent my days learning the boundary between the pulse and the chemical."

Kayla's shoulders eased by a fraction. "The father is a complication I don't care to solve right now. I have made the decision. I am keeping her."

"Her," Jenna repeated.

"The tests were exhaustive. She carries the markers, Mom. The same red-gold codes. The genetic counselor called it 'atypical pheromonal receptor sensitivity.' A long name for a predatory inheritance."

The silence in the room became heavy, a medium thick enough to swim in. The synthesis pathway in Jenna's lungs continued its tireless construction, ignored but absolute.

"She will smell the rot of lies," Jenna said.

"The counselor mentioned the sulfur sensitivity," Kayla whispered. She looked at the river, her eyes tracking the patient indifference of the water. "Imagine growing up in a world where you cannot unsee the truth. Where you smell the ambivalence in a kiss. Where love stinks of uncertainty."

Jenna felt the words like a tectonic shift. She looked at her daughter and finally understood the cost of her own absence. The Raleigh bloodline didn't just offer the sight of the swarm; it offered the weight of knowing everything about the people who were supposed to be the horizon. Jenna hadn't just been a scientist; she had been a frequency Kayla could never quite tune out.

"She'll have you," Jenna said, her voice anchoring the room. "You lack the stench of hesitation."

Kayla considered the glass walls, the shifting light of the gorge. "The rest of the world is a blur of grey, but she is distinct. My conviction only has one focal point."

They sat within the transparency of Dale's vanity. In this box of light, pretense was a ruinous expense. The biometric shackle emitted a dry, electronic pulse—a heartbeat recorded for a ledger in some distant corporate office—then fell silent.

"You're a mirror for the dead," Kayla whispered. "The old photos of Richard. You possess the room before you move through it, as if the air itself has surrendered its secrets to you."

"The compound provides a sensory map," Jenna admitted. "A colonial awareness. I am trying to determine where the chemicals end and my own soul begins. I have spent the last week learning the rhythm of the overlap."

"Does the distinction offer any comfort?"

"It offers a boundary." Jenna looked at her daughter—the armored jacket, the stillness of a girl who had become a sentinel, the granddaughter a hidden pulse eight weeks deep into the world. "I leave for Bethesda tomorrow."

The silence that followed was heavy, a thick medium of unsaid things. "The man from the basement," Kayla finally said.

"Webb. He is the keeper of the rot. He possesses the archive of every woman they harvested before me. He knows the coordinates for a tomb in Hokkaido where a woman named Tanaka might still be breathing. I must claw those records back before the Merck authorization locks the doors. I have nine days before the truth becomes a trade secret."

"And after Bethesda?"

"Then I'll know the true function of what I am becoming." Jenna met the girl's stare. "I will return. This isn't a promise—I am finished with the vanity of timelines I cannot govern. It is a statement of intent. Hold me to it."

Kayla looked through her, her gaze possessing the sharp, refractive gift of the Raleigh line. "You look like you're preparing a calculated descent into the abyss."

A laugh escaped Jenna before she could catch it, the harmonics of the pheromone catching on the glass walls and returning as a layered, buzzing resonance. "Benevolence and catastrophe share the same skin when the stakes reach this height. It is a planned stupidity."

Kayla did not smile, but she did not flinch. "Is this a crusade for the many, or a desperate grab for the relevance you left in the lab?"

The question was a blade, forged in love and whetted by the girl's refusal to lie.

"The altruism and the ego have fused," Jenna said. "I can no longer distinguish the pulse of the hero from the thrum of the survivor. I have accepted the tangle."

Kayla offered a single, sharp nod, filing the answer away. She rose and adjusted the seal of her jacket, a habitual retreat into her own skin. At the threshold of the foyer, she stopped, framed by the dying afternoon.

"What do I tell her? When the bees start calling to her marrow? What is the story of this?"

Jenna watched the light catch the river far below. "Explain that a man once dedicated four decades to a singular, humming devotion. He looked at something he loved until the world changed its shape for him. Tell her the clarity is a burden, but it is the only way to navigate the fog of everyone else's lies. It is a gift that requires an honest hand."

Kayla held the thought, a silent weight. "Okay. Come back."

She vanished into the dusk. Jenna watched the car's tail-lights bleed into the trees at the gate, the only stable anchor in a life defined by tectonic shifts. She sat in the glass cage while the synthesis pathway continued its industrial construction in her blood. She realized then that the granddaughter growing in the dark deserved a world where her awareness was a tool, not a sentence of isolation. That was the foundational truth, the one that remained after the pheromone stopped whispering its urgency.

Midnight arrived like a shroud.

Jenna entered the suit. She did not do it to flee—the biometric shackle still governed her geography, and the house was a minefield of infrared intent. But the armor had become a cognitive lens. Its presence in her awareness had shifted from a garment to a second skeleton. Inside the chrysalis of the helmet, the HUD painted the world in the grammar of heat and intention. The exoskeleton clicked into place, providing the mental focus she needed to finally step into the dark.

Jenna ran the suit through the pre-departure liturgy, a sequence of checks salvaged from the Freedom Fighters' operational manual. She had memorized the text at nineteen, her fingers tracing the actual paper, stained and heavy with the ink of Richard's shorthand. He had never distributed the document; the steel mills of Pittsburgh had claimed him before the team could learn his secrets. Those marginalia—scrawled cautions on the geometry of focus and the weight of the air—were now the primary dialect of her internal thoughts. Richard had understood that knowledge lived in the marrow long before it reached the page. *Be still before you are fast*, he had scratched into the border of the observation protocol. *The bees know when you're ready before you do. Trust the knowing.*

The suit's sensors interrogated her biology with a predatory precision. It catalogued the construction site that was her body: the synthesis pathway hummed with an industrial rhythm, the hexagonal reinforcement was fortifying the calcium of her frame, and the compound eyes had fused with her neural lattice. Her pheromone production sat at a stable, terrifying high. The suit's verdict arrived in a digital rasp: *Significantly beyond prior operational baseline. Recommend field assessment before deployment.*

Jenna found the assessment reasonable. The horizon was Bethesda. The tools: a bus ticket, cash, a hat, a burner phone, and the suit compressed into its hard-shell skin. She would move before the first light hit the gorge. Not through the flagged zones or the monitored thresholds, but through the singular blind spot she had catalogued on her first night. There were fourteen inches of dead space between the garage sensor's reach and the shackle's perimeter—a corridor of silence accessible only through the east hallway window.

For five days, she had scoured her mind of the plan, keeping her thoughts shallow to avoid triggering the biometric alerts of the monitor. She allowed herself to look at it now. With the exoskeleton's neural integration, the planning felt less like effort and more like an extension of her own nervous system. The hard case. The gap. The four-block walk to the station before Rosa's key turned in the lock. Ricky was in position, his message a short, encrypted pulse of safety. Webb was waiting in the Maryland dark, a ghost sitting on two decades of corporate sin.

The bees were active tonight. She felt them through the glass—the wild colonies and the local swarms that had tracked her pheromonal signature from the Florida heat to this river valley. They clung to the birch trees like heavy, dark fruit, building a patient presence around the house. They didn't try to breach the transparency; they simply waited, oriented toward her frequency. They were present, ready, and silent, like the mechanical Michael once tucked into Richard's belt-buckle compartment. They were a resource she didn't yet need to deploy, but their weight was a comfort.

She leaned into the sensation, keeping the pheromone's roar at a manageable level. The synthesis continued its work. The monitor on her ankle dutifully transmitted her elevated pulse to a server in Delaware, feeding data to men who believed they were watching a production facility. They were technically correct, but they lacked the context of the harvest.

The Red Bee was done being kept. It wasn't a dramatic rupture or a cinematic moment of defiance. There was no need for a costume or an audience. It was a cold, structural resolution. She had a plan, and she would execute it with the predatory patience Richard had practiced for forty years. She had spent a lifetime learning that stillness was the highest form of action.

She deactivated the suit's HUD and felt the red dawn in her vision recede to a dull ache. She removed the helmet and lay down in the guest room, watching the Columbia move beneath the floorboards. The pheromone had stolen her need for sleep, replacing it with an electric, humming efficiency, but she chose to close her eyes anyway.

She did not sleep. But she remained perfectly still, and for the first time in weeks, the stillness belonged to her. The river moved. The clock ticked. Four blocks away, a bus was warming its engine for the 6:15 AM departure.

Jenna Raleigh was ready.

Chapter Six: The Swarm

Fourteen inches of unregistered silence existed between the cage and the leash.

Jenna had mapped this hairline fracture in the surveillance during the first hour of her confinement. While the monitor logged her pacing as the aimless agitation of an insomniac, her compound eyes were performing a cold titration of the hallway's dimensions. Geometry had become a functional language. To a beehive, a wall is not an aesthetic boundary; it is a structural datum. Her new vision rendered the world in a frequency where depth and edge were a predatory grammar. She saw the fourteen-inch corridor where the monitor's flagged perimeter failed to overlap with the garage's internal security node—a glitch in the architecture of her imprisonment.

She breached the gap at 4:47 AM. The air was thick with the pre-dawn damp of the Pacific Northwest, a heavy moisture that had warped the old wooden window frame just enough to make it complicit. It yielded without a shriek. She didn't bother looking for the poetic irony in Dale's design choices; time was the only resource currently trading at a premium.

The hard-shell case sat in its impounded purgatory between a pressure washer and a rack of road bikes—hollow monuments to Dale's unlived hobbies. Jenna reached into the unregistered space, her arm extended at a jagged, bone-straining angle to accommodate the case's center of gravity. The physical protest of her muscles was merely a data point to be filtered and discarded.

She slipped back through the window. In the guest room, a pile of laundry lay on the bed, arranged with a desperate, precise mimicry of a human thermal signature. It was a crude ghost meant to satisfy the monitor's appetite for a heartbeat. She dressed in the dark, her movements rhythmic and certain.

Outside, the birch trees held a satellite warmth. She felt the colonies before she saw them—a quiet, patient choir of wings oriented toward her frequency. She didn't command them to follow. To ask for an escort was to risk a signature she couldn't yet mask. They remained in the birches, a living shadow at the property line. Jenna walked the four blocks to the bus station under the weight of the case and the heavy, humid silence of her own history. She didn't look back at the glass house. Looking back invited the rot of nostalgia.

At 6:15 AM, the bus pulled away, a steel lung exhaling onto the highway.

Webb's basement was a sanctuary of dying frequencies. It carried the scent of eroding paper and the sharp, ozone tang of equipment that had been humming since the Cold War. The Faraday caging functioned like a sudden deafness; stepping through the threshold, Jenna felt the abrupt excision of the world's electromagnetic noise. The cellular static, the Wi-Fi pulses, and the rhythmic thrum of the surveillance grid vanished. It felt like shedding a coat made of lead.

Webb was a man who had traded physical space for the density of his secrets. He was smaller than the gravity of his voice suggested—a collapsed star of an operative who had occupied this subterranean void for twenty years. He moved through the banker's boxes with the mechanical efficiency of a librarian tending to a cemetery. He'd memorized the geography of his sins.

He studied her eyes with a clinical, heavy stare. "You're accelerating," he said.

"Eight to thirteen days until the synthesis is absolute," Jenna replied. She set the hard-shell case down with a possessive, instinctive care. It was no longer gear; it was a limb. “The Merck prototype acted as a catalyst. It forced the timeline.”

“Ricky is a clever boy,” Webb muttered, though there was no warmth in the observation. He gestured toward the forty-seven boxes—the paper-bound autopsy of a corporate era. “The Vladivostok files are in the east stacks. But before you touch the skin of that evidence, you need to understand the shape of the beast.”

“Show me,” she said.

He pulled a manila folder from a box marked in Richard’s old shorthand. He slid a photograph across the table: the Eastern Fish Processing Plant. It was a brutalist scar on a Vladivostok pier, its scale far exceeding the aerial maps Ricky had managed to scrape from the public web.

“Stinkov is no longer a freelancer,” Webb said, his voice a dry rasp in the silence. “His operation has metastasized. The fish plant serves as a primary culture facility for a global network of variant deployments. He is the screen, a visible monster for the cameras to focus on while the real phantoms move in the dark. However, he remains the only accessible node holding the parent compound in its uncorrupted state.”

“I need that strain,” Jenna said. She spoke without the tremor of doubt. “The modified variants are echoes. To finish the counter-production protocol, I need the voice. If I don't secure the original biochemical template, the Hokkaido facility and Tanaka’s survival become moot points. Without the source, we are just treating symptoms.”

Webb nodded, a slow, structural movement. “I’ve waited two decades for someone with enough iron in their blood to realize that. Destroying Stinkov is easy. Securing his work before the fire takes it is the only justice worth the cost.”

She reached for the folder. The paper felt like a debt she was finally ready to settle. “Tell me about the security at the pier.”

“The pier is the easy part,” Webb said. “The freezer is where the nightmares are kept.”

The photograph was a window into a frozen throat. Jenna traced the lines of the Vladivostok plant, feeling the narrow space where her own becoming met the system’s failure to contain her. “Who else stalks this ground?”

Webb’s face tightened, the skin pulling like dry parchment over a secret. “You caught the scent.”

“Three weeks of inhaling the chemical ghosts of others has sharpened my senses. The environmental assessment for that pier wasn't a public service; it was a stake in the ground. The corporate shell that cleared the transfer belongs to a rival. They aren’t Sweetwater, but they breathe the same air.”

“Meridian Biosystems,” Webb said, sealing the folder with the funereal care of an undertaker. “They filed the original patents. They’ve orbited Stinkov for fourteen months, waiting for the fruit to ripen. Their hunger for the parent compound matches yours, though their feast will be a different kind of slaughter.”

“Then the race has a second shadow.”

“You must arrive before the predators collide.” Webb looked at her over his spectacles—relics of the nineties that sat on his bridge like iron sentinels. He didn't believe in replacing tools that still held their edge. “Must I remind you of the mortality in this venture?”

“Skip the eulogy,” Jenna said. “Tell me the layout. Map the servers and the deep-freeze where the parent cultures hibernate. I will handle the rest.”

Webb spoke, and Jenna didn't listen with her ears alone. She engaged the suit's memory, her pheromonal drift translating his words into a biochemical script. It was a carving in the marrow, a storage method far more permanent than ink.

She remained in that subterranean vault for four hours, her nervous system absorbing the missing sequences of her own synthesis. When she finally ascended, the world had moved on without her. The afternoon light had turned heavy and bruised, a reminder that time was a predator she couldn't outrun.

"The granddaughter," Webb said as she reached the exit. His voice carried the crushing weight of twenty years of silence. "The markers are there. You've seen the map."

"I know."

"She'll need a shepherd," he whispered. "A teacher to show her how to look at the world without flinching. Richard had four decades to find his peace. You have a handful of days."

"I'll work with the time I'm given," Jenna replied. "I'm coming back for her." She spoke with the iron of intention, leaving the uncertainty of the future for lesser souls.

The tickets were a testament to Ricky's quiet desperation. Twenty-eight thousand dollars a year—a pittance eroded by taxes, fees, and the high-performance hardware he'd bought to keep pace with her evolution. Economy class to Beijing. Seventeen hours in a constricting lung of aluminum and recycled breath. She didn't apologize for the cost; an apology was a shallow coin. Instead, she added his sacrifice to the ledger of debts she intended to settle in blood or brilliance.

The seats were a vice of cheap fabric and human density. In the economy cabin, the world was a sweating mass of data. She inhaled the landscape of the plane: the traveler in 24C was a walking storm of cortisol, his honesty decaying under the strain of a two-year lie regarding his failing heart. In 27-29, a child's chemistry was a burst of clean light, a scent like rain on a parched field. Across the aisle in 25A, there was a hole in the air—a passenger who smelled of nothing. It was the sterile blankness of a professional operative, a man whose biology had been scrubbed and suppressed.

She mapped him with her lateral vision, her compound eyes parsing the edges of her world while she appeared to stare at nothing. He was masked by a management book, but the sulfur of his purpose leaked through the cracks. He was a sentinel, a placeholder.

Not my kill, she decided. *Not yet.*

She turned to the window, watching the Atlantic dissolve into the vast, brown indifference of the Asian steppe. Ricky spoke for hours about the abstract mathematics of digital currency, his voice a restful hum in a world of high-frequency threats. He genuinely loved the logic of the machine, a trait that made him the only tether she had left to the human baseline.

In the Beijing transit terminal, under lights that flickered with the rhythm of institutional decay, she locked herself in a stall and looked at the mirror.

The red had vanished from her eyes. The transformation had moved deeper. Her sclera had been replaced by a refractive sheen, a renovation of the optical frame that bent light into spectra the humans hadn't named. Her pupils were wide voids in the dimness, narrowing into predatory needles when the glare hit. She had become a ghost in a hat and sunglasses, projecting a focused calm to hide the storm of her perception.

She took the glasses off. The mirror reflected a stranger who had looked into the sun for too long. She looked like a woman who had spent her life staring into the shadows and finally learned how to see the things that preferred to remain hidden.

The Trans-Siberian wasn't a voyage; it was a rhythmic siege through the frozen ghost of a continent. Rebranded for the frantic vanity of the digital age, the rail line promised the "greatest journey," yet delivered four days of steel-clad confinement. Outside, the birch forests formed a repetitive white blur against a pewter sky. Inside, the cabin became a closed lung, heavy with the metallic tang of unventilated humanity. The scent of bodies cycling through stale air was an unwanted, perpetual dialogue.

Jenna parsed the passengers like a ledger of suffering and deceit. In car seven, a German backpacker broadcast a sharp, mineral anxiety—the scent of flight from a nameless predator. In car three, two suits traded lies, their competing pheromones clashing in a sour discord of bad-faith negotiation. Then there was the grandmother in car five; her grief had moved past the acute stage and fossilized into something structural. It was no longer an emotion but a skeletal frame she inhabited. Jenna catalogued these signatures with the cold indifference of a sensor, gathering data points in a world made of meat and intentions.

The man in car four was a recurrence. Not the same face from the Dulles flight, but the same signature of artificial stillness—a protocol-born void. He didn't smell of Sweetwater; he carried the oily, aggressive stench of Meridian Biosystems. The corporate vultures who held the original patents were finally circling the carrion. He was watching Stinkov, which meant he needed the parent strain to remain intact as much as she did. They were rivals in a zero-sum game, tethered by a shared target. She left him to his own slow orbit. She wasn't a costumed savior today; she was a biological forge with seven days before her blood completed its redesign.

"He's still there," Ricky whispered, his eyes never leaving the laptop screen. "Hasn't moved since the border crossing."

"He won't," Jenna replied, her voice a low vibration. "He's counting on us to do the heavy lifting. He's a scavenger waiting for the kill."

Ricky slept eventually, his mouth agape in the innocent slackness of a man who hadn't yet learned to edit his own biology. Jenna watched his reflection in the dark glass, her mind drifting to Kayla and the eight-week-old pulse in her daughter's womb. The child would inherit this "curse"—the marker that made the world loud and honest. Kayla feared the isolation of it, but Jenna saw the pivot point. It wasn't a wall; it was a lens. The isolation was merely the noise of the world falling away, leaving only the cold truth of the signal. The girl wouldn't just hear the lies; she would inhabit the primal lexicon of the nerves. She would know the difference between the sulfur of a malicious intent and the musk of a terrified self-preservation.

The train slipped past a cluster of timber hovels that lacked a name on any modern map. They were structures that existed in the deeper current of human persistence, antedating the empires that claimed them. Jenna felt the resonance of the continuity there—the way a body remembers a path it hasn't walked. The bee knows the keeper not by the mask he wears, but by his frequency. She no longer feared the inheritance blooming in her marrow. She was finally tuning herself to the song.

Vladivostok arrived as a monument to entropy and concrete. November had drained the light from the sky, leaving a grey canopy that pressed against the rusted husks in the harbor. The taxi ride through the industrial sprawl was a sensory battering of diesel and brine. Then, the sternum-pull hit. It wasn't a thought but a tectonic orientation. Three kilometers northeast, through the labyrinth of warehouses, the parent compound called to its child. The synthesis pathway in her blood pulsed in sympathy with its root.

Ricky remained oblivious to the biological siren, buried in his phone as he merged satellite maps with the digital ghosts of Stinkov's footprint. He was shedding the skin of the academic, his fingers moving with the rhythm of an insurgent.

"The warehouse is at the end of the pier," Ricky said, his voice tight. "No guards on the perimeter, but the heat signatures are through the roof. He’s running a massive cooling system."

"He's keeping the source alive," Jenna said, her eyes fixated on the distant piers. "Stinkov is an artist of the microscopic. He won't let his masterpiece wither."

"And the Meridian man?"

"He’s behind us. Let him watch. He wants to see how the bee stings."

The hotel wore its ruin like a fashion choice, an inventory of failed intentions where the plumbing groaned with the weight of unfulfilled promises. Ricky had dissected the Wi-Fi within minutes, identifying a digital gill breathing for three separate intelligence agencies—two local shadows and one oily Meridian ghost. Jenna spent thirty minutes submerged in a precise thermal degree of water, a heat that made the buzzing in her blood retreat into a simmer without extinguishing the fire. She stood by the glass with a towel draped over her shoulders, watching the harbor where rusted ships performed a slow, rhythmic argument with the horizon.

Ricky’s knock was a sharp intrusion. “He’s active. Two posts in the last hour,” he said through the heavy wood. “A Patreon update. New cultures are live. He says the donor threshold has been satisfied.”

“The harvest begins a new cycle.” Jenna dressed while her eyes remained locked on the grey water. “What’s the power draw at the plant?”

“Eighteen months of uninterrupted consumption,” Ricky replied. “The grid logs suggest a heart that never stops beating. If he’s keeping the parent cultures in that freezer—”

“He is.” The scent hit her even here, three kilometers of industrial rot and salt-spray away. It was the unadulterated marrow of the strain, the original sin of her biology. “Stinkov understands that the modified variants are brittle ghosts. The parent compound is the only truth he has left. It’s his only leverage against the void.”

She turned from the window, her pulse a hammer. She was already moving.

The Eastern Fish Processing Plant had been hollowed out in 2019, a victim of a privatization scheme that used paperwork as a burial shroud. What remained was the skeleton of industrial intent—loading docks for trucks that had long ago turned to rust, and processing lines of stainless steel maintained with the obsessive devotion of a man who viewed his tools as a liturgy.

The chain-link fence, crowned with jagged wire, was a mere formality. Jenna scaled the mesh before her mind could offer a rationale, her fingers mapping the lattice with the instinctive certainty of her new vision. She didn't see handholds; she felt the grammar of the ascent. The barbed wire at the summit did not snag her skin; it conceded. It felt as though the physical world was beginning to recognize her frequency, yielding to her passage as the sawgrass had at Gator Hole. The universe was becoming a series of open doors.

Ricky followed with the clumsy, heavy effort of a man still bound to a singular human biology. Jenna waited in the shadows of the perimeter, her senses reaching out. She could taste the air; they were alone for the moment. The Meridian operative was either circling the eastern flank or had stalled in his own calculations. She didn't wait to find out.

The generator’s thrum vibrated in her teeth before it reached her ears—a low-frequency growl of machinery fighting the rot of the pier. The freezer occupied the western heart of the plant, a repurposed tomb of cold storage held at a constant, biting minus eighteen Celsius.

Inside, the former cold room was a cathedral of terrariums. They were built from the wreckage of restaurant kitchens and salvaged lab glass, a thousand colonies suspended in an artificial winter. Mosquitoes hung in a state of dreaming malice, their metabolisms slowed to a rhythmic crawl on the edge of extinction. The room was organized with the terrifying neatness of a man who had replaced his soul with a ledger.

Stinkov looked up, his face a map of anticipated triumphs. He was a small man, his fedora tilted at an angle that spoke of a persona built from digital debris. He held a pipette like a scepter. He was smiling.

“The Red Bee,” he rasped. His English was a jagged bridge between clinical precision and the gutter of the internet. “You have aged, Jenna. But the pheromone—you feel the pull, don't you? The mother-tongue of the marrow. I have so many theories regarding the post-reproductive response. I’ve been waiting to dissect a living specimen.”

She didn't offer him the tax of a conversation. She hit him.

She hadn't reached for the suit; the armor was a secondary skin she didn't yet need. Her fist connected with his jaw with the kinetic finality of an insect’s sting. It wasn't a human punch; it was a calibrated release of the hexagonal lattice reinforcing her frame. Stinkov collapsed, the pipette shattering like a crystal prayer against the concrete. The sound rippled through the freezer, a vibration that shook the dormant terrariums and woke the dreaming swarm. A thousand tiny hearts began to beat in time with hers.

Stinkov lay sprawled against the frosted concrete, a smear of crimson blooming on his chin. He wore the grin of a man watching his own house burn and finding the flame patterns aesthetically pleasing.

“Magnificent,” he wheezed. “The aggression response is live. I had concerns the containment protocols had dampened the fire, but you… you are a solar flare.”

“Where are the servers?” Jenna’s voice had lost its singular human focus. It was a chord now, a resonant layering of frequencies that made the air in the freezer feel heavy. The terrariums vibrated in sympathy, the glass humming against the metal racks. It wasn't a request; it was a command issued by the hive.

“The data?” Stinkov touched his jaw, inspecting his teeth for cracks with clinical detachment. “It exists behind that eastern wall. But you miss the point, Doctor. The data is merely a byproduct. The system is the plumbing—the investors, the supply chains, the cold-chain logistics. I am just the gardener. I modify the seeds and document the bloom. The original template? That arrives from elsewhere. I merely harvest the recognition.”

Jenna reached out and hauled him up by the collar. He was lighter than she’d expected, a hollow man buoyed by his own hubris. Her compound eyes parsed his biochemistry in a sudden rush of data: his sweat smelled of frantic excitement and a peculiar, synthesized dopamine. He was leaking the very compound he claimed to curate. He hadn't just lived near the swarm; he’d let it nest in his marrow. He was his own most dedicated test subject.

“Who provides the base?” she demanded.

“I know only the shadows,” Stinkov rasped. His fear was indistinguishable from a sexual thrill, a jagged chemical spike that told Jenna he was already lost to the feedback loop. “The funding arrives through shell companies. It flows like water. This is a commodity, Dr. Raleigh. This is the ultimate consumer good. We have A/B tested the human soul for maximum engagement. The Rage Factor wasn't built for conquest. It was built for visibility.”

He stopped, his pupils dilating until the grey of his eyes vanished. He peered into the slit-pupils of the woman holding him.

“Interesting,” he whispered.

She dropped him. She didn't let him fall; she discarded him like a piece of used equipment. The word *interesting* echoed through the freezer, vibrating in the marrow of her knuckles.

Interesting.

Not a threat. Not a variable. Just a spectacle. She realized then that "interesting" was the trap. It was the lure that had claimed Richard Raleigh and every woman who followed. The system didn't want to conquer the extraordinary; it wanted to farm their ability to be watched. It harvested the light they gave off while it burned them for fuel. She had spent eight years trying to be invisible—taking the adjunct positions, filing the taxes, keeping the armor in a box. But the system had found her at mile marker 23 because she was a high-yield asset. She was a resource to be mined until her heart failed from the sheer friction of being seen.

She turned away from him and walked through the door into the eastern wing. She didn't look back for Ricky. The boy belonged to a world of ethics and sunlight, and she was stepping into the dark belly of the machine.

The server room was a tomb of high-frequency computation. It had once stored ice to keep fish from rotting; now it housed the digital records of human decay. Two rows of black racks groaned under the weight of petabytes. The cooling fans produced a white noise that felt like a permanent scream.

The organizational logic was terrifyingly neat. Research variants were cross-indexed by target demographic: urban clusters, post-industrial flyover zones, religious enclaves. There were blueprints for HVAC dispersal and diagrams for the electromagnetic triggers used in social media feeds. This was the manufacture of a collective fever, a blueprint for a world that only felt alive when it was screaming.

Jenna initiated the download. She refused to read the files as they streamed into her encrypted drive. She had seen what happened to the others—how the data became a mirror, turning the researcher into a specimen. She stayed a predator. She was the hand in the dark, not the eyes on the screen.

"Jenna."

Ricky stood in the doorway, his silhouette framed by the blue light of the servers. His scent was a sharp cord of warning.

"We have to set the failsafe," he said, his voice tight with the realization of where they were. "Stinkov has a remote wipe trigger. He's going to burn the evidence before we can pull it out."

Jenna looked at the console, then back at the freezer door. The swarm in her blood was silent now, coiled and waiting.

"Let him try," she said, her voice vibrating the floorboards. "He thinks he's the one holding the match. He doesn't realize we're the fuel."

She looked back. Through the open door of the server room, Stinkov was a broken idol in a walk-in tomb. He sat amidst the frost, phone clutched in a bloodied hand, his expression a singular, twisted fusion of a man who knew he had lost and a content creator still calculating how to monetize the wreckage.

"Execute it," she said.

Ricky was already deep into the management terminal. His fingers moved with a rhythmic, digital violence, fueled by the particular manner in which people excel at the paths they choose rather than the ones they inherit. He had walked into her lab two years prior because he believed in saving bees; since Florida, he had made a sequence of choices that were entirely his own. Jenna realized she had been leaning on these choices without giving them a name. They weren't just helpful; they were a transformation.

"It's done," Ricky said. His voice had the flat resonance of a closed circuit. "If he touches a wipe command, a digital parasite awakens. It will vomit the entire Sweetwater genealogy to every news desk and terminal on the planet. The front companies, the patent trails, the exact chronology of every deployment." He looked up, the blue light of the monitors etching hard lines into his face. "The engagement metrics too. And the proof that they built the antidote before they ever released the plague."

"Good." She watched the progress bars on her own screen. The data didn't just move; it flowed through her awareness like a dark, informational tide. "Get to the exit. I need two minutes."

"Jenna—"

"Move." The harmonics in her voice weren't a command so much as the hive's honest assessment of the room's atmosphere: she was no longer safe to be near. Ricky understood. He retreated, his footsteps fading into the distance. The freezer door hissed open and shut, followed by a momentary rush of air that smelled of oxidized iron and the peculiar, biting essence of Vladivostok in November—a world so deeply wedded to the frost that warmth felt like a transient lie.

She finalized the download and killed the terminal. For a heartbeat, she stood in the silence, the only sound the white noise of the cooling fans. She let herself understand that what she held was no weapon. It was evidence—the singular currency she had ever trusted. She had it now.

Stinkov was already performing for his digital congregation when she stepped back into the freezer.

He held the phone like a ritual blade, his chin smeared with red, positioning himself against the terrariums with the instinctive eye of a man who understood that background was a form of grammar. He was narrating the encounter in the jagged vocabulary of his cult. She caught the fragments as she passed: *Hive queen. Biohazard thot.* The comments on his screen were a frantic crawl of donations and bile. Thousands of spectators, huddled behind screens, were drinking in the scene from a frozen fish plant in the Russian Far East, waiting for the blood to flow or the world to burn.

She looked at the lens. She did not break it. She did not pose. She looked at it with the compound eyes' terrifying focus—a gaze that ignored the frame to see the desperation beneath. She understood then that her visibility was a structural necessity of the system. She couldn't hide, but she could redirect the current.

She walked past him, a ghost of cold and iron. She moved out of the freezer and onto the plant's main floor, past the silent, stainless-steel skeletons of the processing lines. The November air rushed through the open loading bays, salt-heavy and sharp. The cold clung to her suit case as she walked, her every breath a visible ghost in the dim light of the harbor.

Behind her, the stream hummed on. Whatever Stinkov claimed, whatever metric the system extracted from the image of the Red Bee walking away, she let it go. The colony does not pause its labor to watch a predator retreat. It assesses. It remembers. It returns to the work of building.

The harbor was a landscape of pewter and rust, crowded with ships in various stages of decay or rebirth. Ricky waited by the pier, his distinct chemical signature a blend of terror and resolve. Jenna set the hard-shell case down, looking out at the water with the quiet intensity of two people who had survived a terrible room and remained, somehow, whole.

“The parent strain,” she said. “We need to extract the samples before Meridian closes the circle. Their man is still on the board.”

“I know. I took photos of the terrarium labels while you were in the servers.” He paused, his breath hitching slightly. “I also took a culture. From the oldest unit—the original FSB trial strain. It’s in the case, inner compartment. Sealed and stabilized.”

She looked at him. The compound eyes performed their dual function, layering the biochemical truth over the physical form. Ricky Moraes, twenty-four, a man who had signed up for entomology and ended up in the cold of Vladivostok with enough evidence to dismantle a pharmaceutical empire. He had operated without a protocol, guided only by a chosen courage.

“You’re getting a raise,” she said. “Eventually. When the grant money isn't a digital ghost.”

“I’ll hold you to that.” He picked up his bag, his shoulders squaring. “The train back to Beijing leaves at eleven.”

They walked toward the perimeter fence. The Meridian operative from Car 4 was somewhere in the industrial shadows to the east, hunting the same ghost. He would find the ruins of

Stinkov's vanity and a failsafe that could not be undone. Jenna didn't care. Truth was a slow-moving tectonic plate; it would crush everything in its path eventually.

She scaled the fence with a fluid, predatory grace. The barbed wire didn't snag; it parted like a curtain, an eerie deference that she noted without the tax of a metaphor. The world was simply learning to get out of her way.

The November air was a whetstone for the synthesis pathway. Eight days. Perhaps nine. The timeline was no longer a guess but a rhythmic, industrial certainty. She possessed the parent strain, the encrypted rot of the Sweetwater archives, and a twenty-two-hour transit back to a basement in Bethesda where the truth was waiting to be weaponized. Somewhere between the hotel's broken plumbing and the freezer's artificial winter, she had stopped pretending the Red Bee was a costume. It was the architecture of her survival.

Ricky caught up to her on the industrial road, their breath forming twin ghosts in the dark. The harbor lights shattered across the black water, a thousand jagged reflections that had lived there longer than any empire.

"The man in Car 4," she said, her voice vibrating with a chordal resonance. "He'll be waiting on the return leg."

Ricky adjusted his pack, his scent a steady anchor of resolve. "How do we handle a Meridian shadow?"

"We don't," Jenna replied. "He is a scavenger tracking a scent. Our horizon is wider than his hunger."

They moved toward the city's concrete heart. Behind them, in the bowels of the plant, Stinkov was still performing for his digital hive. The donations ticked upward, a frantic tally of hollow engagement. The system continued to harvest the visible and the loud, feeding on the friction of a world it had set on fire.

But inside Jenna, a different construction was reaching its zenith—a structural, biological rewriting that the system's algorithms hadn't been programmed to see.

She understood now: she wasn't just a victim of the Rage Factor or a witness to the swarm. She was the specific, high-yield problem the system had accidentally built itself to solve.

The harbor was a lung of salt and ice. The bus back to the station was a heartbeat away.

The Red Bee was ready.

Chapter Seven: The Crop

The shadow from car 4 had solidified on the platform.

He didn't wait for them; he waited for the moment. He stood at the far terminus of the Vladivostok station, clutching a kiosk coffee he hadn't tasted. He had positioned himself at a vertex that commanded the entrance gates and the iron veins of the stairs. His suppression protocol was a cold shroud in the Siberian air—a biochemical void that functioned as a fingerprint for those who knew how to read the absence of a soul. He watched their approach through the peripheral static of a professional. Jenna mirrored the movement, a silent dance of predators trained by different masters of the same dark craft.

“Car 4 again,” Ricky whispered, his gaze anchored to the ground.

“A different carriage this time.” She steered him toward the entrance of car 9, the furthest reach of the steel spine. It placed four hundred meters of iron and the rhythmic breathing of sleepers between them and Meridian’s operational clock. “He won’t strike here. The cameras are too numerous, the stage too public. He is outside his net of safety.”

“When?”

“When he confirms the kill.”

The kill was the parent compound, currently nested in the hard-shell case, swaddled in the thermal layers Ricky had scavenged from a local chemist. They held the only leverage that mattered, a secret they guarded with the frantic care of a fading light.

The cabin was a humid contrast to the platform’s bite. The Russian heaters were locked in an ancient, unyielding war with the cold, oblivious to the passengers' needs. Outside, the birch forests were ink-stains against a sky struggling to be born. Jenna sat across from Ricky, watching the gloom dissolve into the skeletal shapes of the taiga. Her mind drifted to the Hokkaido facility—a place of power draws and maintenance ledgers.

Riku Tanaka was a ghost documented by checks and balances. Officially, she had succumbed to respiratory failure twenty-nine months ago—a sanitized corporate eulogy for a production vessel that had reached its limit. But the checks hadn't stopped. The facility had been breathing for thirty-one months. The system doesn't pay for empty rooms. Tanaka was still a factory, her heart a rhythmic engine for BrinCell’s profit. She was the survival evidence Jenna’s blood was currently replicating—the proof that the synthesis could be endured, provided the cage was strong enough.

The train surged through the frozen dark. Ricky surrendered to a shallow sleep. The man in car 4 remained a static point in the distance. Inside Jenna, the pathway continued its tireless weaving, and the former hero watched the birches emerge from the void, contemplating the horror of a life cultivated for a harvest.

⁂

The Beijing transit terminal was a temple of glass and neon, and the news screens had found her before she found them.

The image wasn't the woman she had spent three weeks becoming—the muted scholar in sunglasses and a nondescript hat. It was the titan from the Florida marsh. The visor of her helmet was a jagged map of cracks, her eyes visible through the shards: compound, hemorrhaging a bruised red, the sclera reacting to the high-frequency stress of the world. The camera had looked up at her from the mud, turning her into a towering silhouette of wrongness.

AGING SUPERHERO GONE ROGUE, the crawl screamed in that hollow register of media that had already convicted the accused. **Former Red Bee Implicated in International Incident; Assault, Theft of Proprietary Research Compounds.**

Ricky's stride broke. Jenna didn't slow. She maintained her pace, her eyes fixed on the horizon of the terminal. To stop was to confess. She was a ghost in a crowd, the man from car 4 a sixty-meter anchor behind them.

"The Cybertruck," Ricky said, his voice a frantic vibration as he caught up.

"And the fish plant," she replied. "And whatever Stinkov's ghost-writers are feeding the tabloids." She guided him toward the sanctuary of a concrete pillar, the hard case a weight between her feet. She engaged her peripheral vision, mapping the electronic eyes in the ceiling and the rhythmic movement of the security details. "BrinCell is the author of this warrant. They're using the Vladivostok footage to burn the bridges behind us."

"They've been watching the whole time," Ricky realized.

She had known, but the silence had been a tactical necessity. She filed the omission away—a debt she would have to pay before the synthesis made her something incapable of regret.

"We're taking the Seoul connection," she said. "The direct route is a trap. Seoul buys us two hours before the facial recognition nodes can update the federal blacklists. It's a narrow window, but it's the only one left."

Ricky looked at her then, a long, searching gaze that sought the woman beneath the darkening iris. He didn't flinch. He didn't pull away from the monster on the screen. His biochemistry remained a steady hum of loyalty, a lack of fear that Jenna found more terrifying than the warrants. She couldn't tell him that she had expected him to run. That acknowledgment required a version of herself she wasn't sure still existed.

“Seoul,” he agreed.

The motel in Incheon was a sterile purgatory, a waypoint for the ghosts of the global economy. It offered the minimum requirements for a human frame to pause, a place where time was measured in the arrival of flight crews and the humming of ice machines. Jenna stood in the shower, the door gaped open. Her new biology demanded the perimeter; the compound eyes turned the cramped bathroom into a fragmented mosaic of data. To close the door was to accept a blind spot, and the sensory system now hardwired into her brain regarded an enclosed room as a tactical failure.

Ricky sat on the edge of the second bed, the laptop glowing against the dim, beige walls. He had spent the flight weaving Stinkov’s raw data into the corporate tapestry Webb had provided. He worked with the silent, rhythmic industry of a man who had accepted his role as the architect of the truth.

Jenna stepped out, a towel draped over shoulders that felt increasingly foreign. She stood behind him, looking at the hierarchy of exploitation he had uncovered.

The Rage Factor was merely the loud, discordant overture to a symphony of silence. It was the visible tip of a submerged monolith. Stinkov’s servers didn’t just list a series of drugs; they detailed an operating system for human behavior. The parent compound was the core code; the variants were applications designed to optimize the biological harvest.

“Focus Factor,” Ricky muttered. His voice had the hollow resonance of a man who had looked into the abyss and started counting the teeth. “They didn't just target the labs. They targeted the classrooms. A chemical nudge for Texas school districts. It dampens the fire, narrows the world until only the test remains. It turns children into drones for a week, and when they crash, it leaves a residue of anxiety that Meridian is more than happy to medicate. It's a closed-loop economy of the mind."

"Feeding the beast with one hand and selling the bandage with the other," Jenna said.

"It's everywhere, Dr. Raleigh. 'Workforce Enhancement' in the grease of the food service industry. It's in the laminates of the burger wraps, the polymers of the fry boxes. A transdermal hit of obedience to keep the minimum-wage gears turning. It's been active for six years. We've been living in an experimental hive, and the Rage Factor was just the first time they decided to see how hard they could poke the nest."

Jenna stared at the scrolling columns of numbers. The synthesis pathway in her chest thrummed—a patient, structural vibration. It was indifferent to the horror. It had its own directives: survive, expand, complete. It was more interested in the integrity of her heart than the shattering of her soul.

"Show me the PheroGuard data," she said.

Ricky's fingers hesitated. He pulled up the Merck files. Jenna read the clinical summaries, her eyes parsing the light before it could even hit her retinas. Twenty-three test subjects. All post-reproductive women. All carrying the Raleigh marker. The active ingredient was a proprietary protein harvested from a biological source.

Subject RB-1.

The room grew very cold. Jenna didn't feel it, but she knew the temperature had dropped. "The 72-hour hold," she whispered.

“BrinCell didn't just evaluate you, Jenna,” Ricky said, his voice a thread of grief. “They mined you. They took your blood while you were unconscious and sold the licensing rights to Merck seven weeks ago. The blocker you swallowed to stop the hum... it was built from the marrow they stole from you.”

The realization was a jagged blade in the dark. The inhibitor—the great savior of the coming plague—was her own biology sold back to a world they had poisoned. She was the vector, the victim, and the commercial solution, all refined into a single, profitable cycle.

“Don’t tell me the revenue projections,” she said, moving to the window. The airport access road was a grey ribbon of indifference. “I need the sequence. I need to see the cage from the outside.”

She closed her eyes, but the vision remained. Plans within plans.

The Raleigh line wasn't a heritage; it was a crop. Richard’s forty years of singing to the hive had been a long-term selective breeding program. Her career hadn't been a series of failures; it had been a managed environment. Her grant wasn't denied; it was impounded. Her ex-husband wasn't a man reaching out; he was the trigger, a marionette whose financial strings were pulled by a Palladian shell.

They had grown her in the dark. They had waited for the precise moment when the biology was ripe, then they had whistled for the swarm.

Jenna looked at her reflection in the glass. The hexagonal patterns beneath her skin were no longer an infection. They were the bars of a prison she had helped build with her own dissertation.

“What’s the next move?” Ricky asked.

Jenna turned back to the room. Her pupils were needles of absolute intent. “The sequence is complete. Now we look at the ending they didn't write.”

The sawgrass at Gator Hole hadn’t been a landscape; it was a delivery room. The mosquitoes hadn't found her by the blind luck of a shifting wind. They had Parted for the arrival of a sovereign. Jenna stared at the screen, the blue light reflecting in eyes that now perceived the refresh rate as a rhythmic, agonizing pulse. She understood the nature of the royal jelly now. She hadn't been a victim of a spill or a stray contagion. She was the genetically refined crop, selected and groomed through a decade of managed shadows. They had fed her the conditions for her own bloom, waiting for the precise moment when her biological clock aligned with their industrial intent.

She had spent her life mapping how the hive selects its chosen few. She knew the chemical alchemy that turned a common larva into a queen. The colony never searches for its ruler. It constructs her.

The hotel mattress offered a rigid, institutional resistance against her spine. The discomfort was a tether, a reminder that she still occupied a frame of meat and bone, even as the hexagonal lattice continued to colonize her marrow. She nudged Ricky’s leg with her foot. He stirred, the bioluminescent glow of the laptop casting distorted shadows across his sleeping face.

"I need the genetic sequencing from Stinkov’s servers," she said, her voice a low, vibrating chord. "The susceptibility markers. Give me the full panel. No summaries."

He blinked back the fog of exhaustion, his fingers finding the keys by a learned instinct. He didn't ask why. He simply surrendered the data.

At three in the morning, the truth arrived in a cascade of cold code. Ricky had drifted back into a shallow sleep, his breath a rhythmic counterpoint to the hum of the cooling fan. The screen was a window into a fifteen-year betrayal. The susceptibility marker was a constellation of fifteen distinct genetic variants. Each one was a mundane mutation in isolation, but together, they formed a singular lock.

The targeting system hadn't been built with precision. It had been built with malice. They had used her 2009 dissertation as a production manual, a roadmap to her own nervous system. Fifteen markers for fifteen years of quiet observation. Chen, Okafor, and Tanaka had been the rough drafts—partial matches used to test the tolerances of the strain. Jenna was the finished manuscript. She was the fifteen-for-fifteen expression the compound had been calibrated to ignite.

Dale’s voice echoed in her memory, a hollow, smiling ghost. *Come on, Jenna. You miss the sting.* He hadn't been lying. He had been a tool, his nostalgia and his concern repurposed into a delivery mechanism. They had dosed him weeks before her arrival, not to change him, but to tune him. They had played him like a low-frequency instrument to lure the queen back to the hive. She hadn't been investigating a crime. She had been answering a summons.

The burner phone on the nightstand vibrated, a sharp, plastic rattle. The signal was a thin thread, vibrating through the living tissue of the world. She answered before the second pulse.

"You found the markers," Webb said. It was the voice of a man who had spent too long breathing the air of a Faraday cage.

"All fifteen," Jenna said. "You knew the count."

"I have carried that panel since 2007," Webb replied, the sound of his breath like dry parchment. "I didn't offer it as a briefing because a revelation is only a ghost until you earn the sight of it. You needed to find the blood on the floor yourself. You are a scientist. You require the evidence of the crime before you can prosecute the criminal."

Jenna watched a silver filament drip from her lip onto the hotel carpet. It vanished into the fibers, a predator seeking a dark corner. "The Hokkaido facility. Tanaka is the production template for the PheroGuard inhibitor. They've been keeping her in a state of permanent expiration for thirty-one months."

"Maintaining her," Webb corrected, the word heavy with the stench of a laboratory. "She is the living engine for the late-stage compound. They keep her compliant enough to produce and broken enough to stay. Reaching her means dismantling a fortress designed by men who fear the very things they farm. But reaching her is a tactical gesture, Jenna. It is a scream in a vacuum. The system has your samples. It has the emergency authorizations. It has the market cornered."

"I am not looking for a tactical gesture," Jenna said.

"Then listen to the warning," Webb's voice shifted, the ancient, weary authority of the national id sharpening into a blade. "I was wrong about your rage. I measured it as a fuel, a purposeful fire that wouldn't consume the engine. I stand by that. But the system has mapped the heat of your anger. Look at the Stinkov data. Look at the engagement projections for the Red Bee."

Jenna's fingers moved across the trackpad. She opened the files Ricky had dragged out of the Vladivostok dark. A new set of models populated the screen—simulations of her own rebellion.

"They don't want to stop you, Jenna," Webb whispered. "They want to broadcast you. They modeled the Red Bee as a marketing campaign. Every punch you throw, every corporate laboratory you burn, every dramatic escape—it is all content. You are the visible threat that creates the demand for the cure. Your fury is the advertisement. They have built an entire economic cycle around your refusal to die. They are praying you suit up. They are counting on your anger to sell the antidote to a terrified world."

Jenna stared at the projections. Her own face, stylized and masked, pulsed in a high-frequency loop of manufactured chaos. They had turned her soul into a recurring revenue stream.

"They don't need you to be a subject anymore," Webb said. "They need you to be a hero. Because a hero creates a spectacle, and a spectacle creates a desperate, paying audience."

The data on the screen flickered with the cold, rhythmic pulse of a predatory heart. Jenna watched the projections, her gaze unwavering as she absorbed the meticulous horror of her own obsolescence. The numbers laid bare a truth the pheromones had already whispered to her marrow: she was the catalyst for a global market. The Red Bee, a rogue titan captured on every dashboard camera and cellular feed, served as the ultimate proof of concept. The contagion was real, the chaos was visceral, and the demand for a cure was reaching a fever pitch. BrinCell didn't need to hunt her; they needed to broadcast her. She was the infection and the source of the remedy, a self-sustaining cycle of profit fueled by her own righteous fury.

"The hunt is the harvest," she said, her voice a low, harmonic vibration. The realization coalesced in the dim motel room, heavy as a physical weight. "They won't capture me because a cage kills the narrative. They need me running, breaking things, becoming a monster in the public eye. Every drop of blood I spill is a dividend. Every laboratory I shatter is a commercial for the antidote they're brewing from my veins."

"The market consumes everything," Webb's voice rasped through the speaker, sounding like dry leaves skittering over a tombstone.

"And you're telling me this because I can't just run into the woods. Absence is just another data point for them."

"Correct. The Stinkov models already account for the 'Mystery of the Red Bee.' Silence breeds its own brand of speculation, its own fervor. The engagement economy has a stomach for ghosts. What it cannot digest is the end of the question itself."

Jenna looked toward the window. The Incheon airport road was a ribbon of industrial ash under the four AM sky. The world outside appeared hollow, a stage stripped of its actors, existing only in the margins of a machine that demanded constant tribute.

"Resolution," she murmured.

"The structural dismantling of the lie," Webb replied. "A complete release of the evidence, coupled with a synthesis pathway inhibitor that doesn't belong to a corporation. You must produce the knowledge that makes the commodity irrelevant. This is the only path they haven't mapped. They haven't tried because the compound is designed to keep the host in a state of primitive agitation. Rage is loud. Rage is blind. Rage keeps you from seeing the gears."

"They wanted a beast. They didn't account for the researcher," Jenna said. She looked at her hands. Beneath the skin, the hexagonal lattice of her knuckles hummed with a crystalline stability. The early phase of the infection had been a storm of fire and cortisol, a parasitic hunger for conflict. But the transition had brought a terrifying, frozen clarity. The hive mind was no longer screaming; it was calculating.

"In the laboratory of your own body, the rules have changed," Webb said. "The system expects you to collapse or be contained. It does not expect a subject to achieve a stable state in the wild, governed only by the cold focus you've spent forty years perfecting. You are a biological anomaly, Jenna. A queen who refused the hive's script."

"I'm going to Hokkaido," she said. The decision was not a choice; it was an inevitability.

"I expected as much."

"I’m not going there to break their toys. I’m going to retrieve Tanaka. She has lived in that vault for thirty-one months, a prisoner of their management protocols. If I combine what she has synthesized under their gaze with what I have forged in the wind, we create a total sequence. We bypass their clinical trials. We render their patents worthless."

"The counter-production protocol," Webb whispered. "I have waited twenty years for a mind capable of finishing that sentence. Richard’s blood was always meant for this. It was meant to be a shield, not a product."

"Does Tanaka know I'm coming?"

"She is alive and she is unyielding. That is all the answer you need."

Jenna severed the connection. The room fell into a heavy silence, punctuated only by the shallow, rhythmic breathing of Ricky on the adjacent bed. He lay there with the laptop still propped against his chest, a child playing at war in a world of monsters. She looked at him with a distant, clinical pity, then turned back to the screen.

The terms of the engagement were set. She had seven days before the transition was final, seven days before the window of her human agency was pinned under the weight of the full expression. Seven days while every corporate mercenary and government shadow-unit in the hemisphere closed in on her location.

She opened the facility maps. The power draw at the Hokkaido site was a rhythmic pulse, a heartbeat of high-voltage intent.

She mapped the thermal signatures, the satellite ghosts of a prison built from the wreckage of a research station. She didn't need a weapon. She needed a sequence. She had written a dissertation in six days while her life was falling apart. She could dismantle an empire in seven.

"Wake up, Ricky," she said, her voice vibrating the glass of the window. "We have a plane to catch, and I need you to find me a way into a freezer that doesn't exist on any map."

The anger had sublimated into a lucidity so sharp it felt like a physical edge. It was the state Richard's scribbled notes had promised: the stillness of the hive before the swarm takes flight, a readiness the body recognizes long before the conscious mind catches up. Her compound eyes didn't just see the blue light of the monitor; they parsed the skeleton of a system designed across fifteen years to strip-mine her blood. She watched the data stream, a hunter observing the tracks of a beast that assumed it was invisible. The machine had ignored the biology. It had quantified her as a resource, failing to grasp the patient, evidence-based reality of a living system. She had spent forty-two years learning to trust that truth.

At 5:30 AM, the silence of the motel room shifted. Ricky pushed himself upright, his laptop a dead weight on his chest. He looked around with the disorientation of a man waking in a vacuum.

"You never went under," he said, his voice sandpaper-dry.

"The Hokkaido variables are mapped," Jenna replied, her voice a low vibration that made the cheap glass on the nightstand shudder. "Three contingencies. I've recalibrated the synthesis timeline to account for the blocker's acceleration. We have a supply chain leak for the counter-protocol that your Merck contact needs to plug." She looked at him, her pupils narrowing into vertical slits. "And I know how to move the man from car four. He's a variable I can finally solve."

Ricky stared at her, offering a look she recognized—the silent consent of a man who had already accepted the bill for a war he hadn't planned to join. "Tell me."

She laid it out. He absorbed the complexity without a flinch, his mind integrating the data like a machine. Outside, the Incheon road began to glow with the industrial grey of a morning that had no interest in hope.

"There's a cargo routing service," Ricky said after a long beat. "A dark-net Discord. Shadow logistics. The kind of pilots who don't ask for warrants because they don't believe in maps." He paused, a flicker of guilt crossing his face. "I've had the channel bookmarked since Vladivostok."

Jenna's gaze locked onto him. "You've been holding that back."

"Since before Vladivostok, actually," he confessed, his voice steadying. "Since the ankle monitor. I was building exits while you were building the case. I thought we might need to cross the Pacific without leaving a trail."

She turned back to the screen. The Hokkaido satellite images were a map of a living cage. She saw the power draws, the maintenance payments, the thirty-one months of a heart being forced to beat for the benefit of a pharmaceutical ledger. She thought of the eight-week-old pulse in Kayla's womb—a child destined to enter a world where human emotion was a traded commodity, where a board of directors could patent a granddaughter's tears.

She thought of the mechanical Michael, the ghost in Richard's belt buckle, a tiny engine of purpose held in reserve for half a century.

"Book the flight," she said.

The sun breached the horizon over Incheon with an indifferent, ancient persistence. It rose as it had for eons, unimpressed by the corporate harvest of human attention. Jenna Raleigh—wanted, transformed, seven days from a biological event she could barely name—turned back to the machine.

The synthesis pathway moved through her veins like a tectonic shift, patient and structural. Her blood was building its own truth, answering the directives of the only master who had ever given it what it needed to thrive.

The world looked at her and saw a crop to be gathered. They were wrong.

She was the beekeeper.

Chapter Eight: Full Expression

The cargo routing service occupied a skeletal warehouse district near Incheon's secondary port, a liminal space squatting in the blind spot of customs authorities. It was a cathedral of the overlooked, staffed by men who had turned the study of bureaucratic gaps into a high priesthood. For a fee calibrated to the scent of desperation and paid in a currency that had forgotten the internet's panopticon, they offered passage to the jagged edges of the map—places where standard carriers had been persuaded, through violence or coin, to ignore.

Ricky had unearthed the connection through a splintered Discord server dedicated to the logistics of the impossible. Jenna turned that thought over in her mind, a jagged stone of a sentence that described the world as it truly breathed, rather than the sterilized version she had once expected to inhabit.

The flight spanned eleven hours of rattling industrial transit inside a converted freighter. The cabin air was a thick soup of machine oil and the lingering ghost of a previous cargo. The pilot, a man whose skin looked like cured leather, identified the phantom scent as agricultural equipment without being prompted. He did not ask for their manifesto. Jenna recognized the exchange as a silent liturgy of the trade—she ignored his equipment, he ignored the hard-shell case, and the silence held the functional grace of a system designed by those who knew that some questions carried a price far higher than their answers.

She found no rest in the vibration of the hull. The synthesis pathway had shifted its rhythm two days prior, or perhaps she had simply surrendered to its tempo. The distinction felt increasingly academic. The biological masonry it was erecting in her chest had breached a threshold she could only identify through the rearview mirror of her own evolution; it was the moment a building stops being a frame and becomes a structure the second the final wall seals. Her internal diagnostics, run in the shivering light of an Incheon motel bathroom, had sharpened the horizon. ESTIMATED TIME TO FULL EXPRESSION: 3–5 DAYS.

The math was a cold blade. Eleven hours of air, then the grit of ground transport, then the approach to a facility that held her predecessor's ghost. It was the kind of arithmetic that demanded a perfect alignment of stars, the sort of logic she had abandoned at thirty-six when she finally realized that situations following a plan were the ones that never required a plan to begin with.

She dove into the approach contingencies instead. The satellite imagery, thirty days stale, was a mosaic she corrected against the facility's power consumption. The draw was massive, a rhythmic heartbeat consistent with climate-controlled biological storage and the thermal signature of life-support systems running in a frantic parallel with laboratory guts.

The perimeter offered three punctures. Two showed the scuff of recent gravel displacement—the physical residue of deliveries and the logistics of a contained nightmare. The third, on the north face, remained a silent void. It was a loading dock that dated back to the facility's original skin, before BrinCell had flayed it and remade it in their own image.

Pre-conversion. Before the corporate vultures had moved in, this had been the Hokkaido Prefectural Agricultural Research Station. She had traced the ownership chain through the long hours since Incheon, peeling back layers of privatization and subsidiary shells to find the Aquaculture Research Station decommissioned in 2017. The blueprints were ghosts of a previous life, but they revealed a truth the renovation hadn't dared to erase: the intake pipes.

Water was the facility's breath. If there was water, there was a path for a sting.

She was tracing the veins of the water infrastructure when Ricky stirred. He sat up in the cargo webbing with the efficient, untethered motion of a predator waking from a shallow dream. He looked at her screen, his eyes locking onto the blue line she was following through the north wall.

“That’s two meters below the grade,” he said, his voice a low gravel.

“Aquaculture intake. BrinCell buried the access under the loading dock expansion, but the thermal data doesn't lie.” She pointed to a faint shimmer on the overlay. “The water is moving. The pipe isn't a tomb; it’s being maintained.”

“Why keep a vestigial organ alive?”

“Because it isn't vestigial. The biological cultures they’re farming require humidity cycling that standard HVAC systems can’t simulate without crashing. The old aquaculture connection is their lung.” She looked at him, her pupils narrowing. “That pipe is clear because it’s the only thing keeping their investment from drying out.”

Ricky didn't blink. “How wide?”

“Fifty-two centimeters.”

He looked at her, then at the suit case, measuring the new, sharp angles of her body. He saw the way the synthesis had leaned her out, turning her into something optimized for narrow spaces. “You’ll fit.”

It wasn't a question, but a statement of trust. He went back to his laptop, the cargo netting swaying as the freighter hit a pocket of turbulent air over the Yellow Sea. He returned to the counter-production calculations, his fingers moving in a frantic dance to stay ahead of the clock.

Outside, the Pacific was a black void beneath them, a cold desert of memory holding everything that had ever been swallowed by the deep. Inside, the synthesis pathway hammered the final nails into the new house of her blood.

⁂

The shadow from car 4 had arrived in Sapporo.

She caught the electromagnetic scent of his signal in the Hokkaido cellular grid before they had even cleared the gate at New Chitose. It was a distinctive, artificial silence—a suppression protocol running in a city that had no reason to be quiet. He was forty kilometers north, moving along the expressway at the steady, unhurried pace of a man staging an execution rather than pursuing a target. He was building toward a moment that wasn't yet today.

She looked at the digital clock. She had six hours.

The facility squatted among the agricultural flats of the Tokachi Plain, a landscape of dead straw and a sky that looked like bruised lead. It was a converted greenhouse complex, long and low, its aluminum sides painted in a beige meant to blend into the boredom of the countryside. Chain-link and glass-eyed cameras guarded the perimeter, but they were tools for watching humans, not things that moved through the earth.

The intake pipe was exactly where the old world had left it. It smelled of wet stone and the mineral tang of the water table, but beneath that was the beeswax scent of the facility’s internal cultures. She shed the suit, knowing its bulk would be a liability in the crawl. She moved into the dark as herself, her skin sensing the vibration of the facility’s heart through the concrete. The space was tight—a suffocating, cold embrace—but her body yielded with a new, fluid grace. She wasn't fighting the pipe; she was becoming part of its flow.

She emerged through a floor panel in the maintenance wing, the air inside thick with the taste of a laboratory. It was the smell of a harvest.

She moved through the shadows of the corridor, her vision fracturing into a thousand points of data. She felt the resonance before she saw the person—a vibration in her marrow that matched the frequency of her own blood. Riku Tanaka was thirty meters away, a living lung breathing for the benefit of a corporate ledger.

Jenna reached the end of the lab wing and found the door. Tanaka was sitting at a bench, her back to the entrance. She didn't turn when the door hissed open.

“You’re early,” Tanaka said, her voice a dry rasp. “I had you arriving on Thursday.”

“I didn't take the front door.”

Tanaka turned then, and Jenna saw her own future reflected in the other woman’s eyes. The compound gaze, the hexagonal skin, the look of someone who had lived in the center of a storm for thirty-one months and had decided to stop waiting for it to end.

“The pathway resonance,” Tanaka said, her eyes scanning Jenna with terrifying efficiency. “Three days to full expression? Maybe less.”

“The HUD says three.”

“The HUD is an optimist.” Tanaka looked at the hard-shell case Jenna had dragged through the mud. “You have the parent strain?”

“I have everything. Stinkov’s data, Webb’s archives, the blood of the original.”

Tanaka leaned back, a small, ghost of a smile touching her lips. “Then we stop being the crop. We become the winter.”

The Tokachi Plain in November was a study in desolation, the color of cold straw beneath a bruised sky. The land performed a seasonal ritual of diminishment, a place that had bartered its fertility for the heavy, waiting silence of late autumn. The former research station sat like a barrow in the flats, a converted greenhouse complex whose long, low buildings retained the skeletal profile of agricultural utility. Their aluminum hides had been painted an institutional beige—a hue designed to signal a controlled-access perimeter without the vulgarity of advertising it.

A chain-link fence held the world at bay. At the gate, a guard sat in a vehicle devoid of markings, his attention anchored to the blue-light glow of a phone. The surveillance grid was a textbook exercise in professional arrogance; it covered 343 degrees of the perimeter, leaving a seventeen-degree blind spot at the northeast corner. It was the precise flaw of designers who had optimized for terrestrial threats and failed to account for a subterranean artery.

Jenna left the car four kilometers back, sheltered by a closed farm equipment supplier. Ricky stayed with the hardware, the encrypted channel a thin thread of continuity. He was running the final counter-production modeling, a sequence that required the biological truth hidden inside the beige walls.

"If the Meridian operative moves faster than six hours," she said, her voice a low, harmonic rasp.

"I’ll run the signal protocol," Ricky replied. "You’ll feel it."

She would. The biological network operating beneath the threshold of electromagnetic noise had grown with her synthesis. Even at this distance, she could taste Ricky’s biochemistry—the sharp, mineral tang of an anxiety that had chosen to show up regardless of the cost. The signal would arrive through her marrow, a four-minute warning before the shadow of the hawk fell.

Four minutes was a lifetime for a predator.

She crossed the fields in a rhythmic, low-profile ghosting. Her compound eyes mapped the terrain in frequencies that lacked a human name: the thermal pulse of the soil, the electric hum of the facility's nervous system, the faint, floral warmth of engineered life leaking through the siding. The intake pipe's access point was exactly where the blueprints promised—a minor miracle of physical reality that she noted and discarded. Gratitude was a form of friction.

The pipe was a concrete throat, cold with the deep frost of the water table. It exhaled a damp, organic vapor: the beeswax note of controlled cultures and the metallic scent of iron oxidation. Her forty-two years of professional witness translated the air instantly. The humidity systems were at capacity. The crop was healthy. Whatever they were farming inside was breathing.

She moved through the conduit without the suit; the fifty-two-centimeter bore demanded a body stripped of technology. She navigated by proprioception and the enhanced grace of a nervous system that had spent six weeks being flayed and remade. The fit was accurate rather than comfortable, a cold, concrete embrace that she navigated with the fluid efficiency of a creature returning to a burrow.

The pipe terminated at a junction node—the facility's humidity mixing chamber. She breached the floor access through a bolt that her thermal vision identified as under-torqued. A maintenance shortcut, invisible to a standard inspection, but a glaring invitation to a biology that could read the heat of stressed metal.

She emerged into the interior.

The air was twenty degrees warmer, a heavy soup of mineral growth media and the metabolic exhaust of high-concentration cultures. She stood in the maintenance corridor, allowing her vision to fracture and reassemble the facility's map from the electromagnetic ghosts of the equipment.

Three guards. One at the gate, two in the western administrative wing. Their biochemical signatures were flat, professional, and bored—the slow, rhythmic pulse of men who believed they were alone.

But there was a fourth resonance.

It arrived not as data, but as a chord. It was a frequency that vibrated in the same register as her own marrow, a tuning fork struck in a distant room. It wasn't identical, but it was close—the specific proximity of two versions of the same original sequence running at different stages of expression. It was the hum of shared inheritance.

Riku Tanaka. Alive. Thirty meters away.

Jenna moved through the maintenance corridor, bypassing the water infrastructure with the silence of a shadow. She reached the eastern wing's service door, a portal left unlocked by a security design that prioritized containment over intrusion.

The eastern lab section was a ghost of its former self. Benches and fume hoods remained, but they were now draped in the sterile, negative-pressure lungs of BrinCell's containment. The system was designed to keep airborne variants from escaping, a unidirectional flow that assumed the threat was a gas. It hadn't accounted for a researcher who had spent thirty-one months memorizing the environmental architecture of her cage. Tanaka hadn't just been a specimen; she had been the architect of her own margins.

Jenna saw the evidence of it immediately: notes etched into the condensation of the glass, chemical traces on the benches that were not part of the facility's production. Tanaka had been conducting a slow-motion rebellion in the very air she breathed.

Jenna recognized the signature of the work instantly. It was a phantom methodology, a sequence of ghosts conducted in the margins of a cage. She had lived that same rhythm in the glass rectangle above the Columbia, matching the cadence of her breath to the blink of a smoke-detector camera. Tanaka hadn't been waiting for a savior; she had been terraforming her own biology.

Notes were etched into the condensation on the lab windows, a frost of data. Chemical traces lingered on the bench surfaces—substances that were not in the BrinCell inventory. Tanaka had been cultivating her own counter-agent within the medium of her own flesh, using the very compound meant to enslave her as a fuel for her liberation.

The room at the end of the eastern wing was a cavernous laboratory repurposed as a stable. It was climate-controlled with a clinical apathy—just comfortable enough to keep the asset breathing, but too barren to allow it to feel human.

Tanaka was sitting at the bench, her back to the service door. She was bent over a culture sample, peering through improvised optics she had cannibalized from the facility's inspection gear. Her hair was a jagged, utilitarian crop, shorter than her last file photo. She did not startle when the door hissed open. She sat in a terrifying, heavy stillness, her biochemistry radiating a resonance that Jenna had felt while still inside the intake pipe.

"You're earlier than I calculated," Tanaka said. She didn't turn. "I had you arriving on Thursday."

"We found a shortcut through the plumbing."

"I assumed." Tanaka set down the optics. "I could feel you in the concrete. The pathway resonance—it's louder than I expected. How many days?"

"Three to five, according to the HUD."

Tanaka turned then. Jenna saw the eyes—the multifaceted, refractive architecture of the Red Bee, but matured. It was a face she had known only from an old, grainy photograph, now rendered in the sharp reality of a transformation thirty-one months deep. The sclera had become a bruised, deep violet; the hexagonal facets of the cornea caught the flickering fluorescent light like diamonds.

"Three to five days," Tanaka murmured. Her voice lacked the frantic heat of the early stages. It was a cold, precise vibration. "That's faster than anyone else has reached it without controlled conditions. The wild synthesis is more efficient than BrinCell predicted." She studied Jenna with a mutual, biochemical processing—an introduction that required no lies. "How long since Gator Hole?"

"Six weeks."

"I was eight months in the cage before I peaked." Tanaka offered no inflection, but her eyes darkened. "The controlled conditions were not, as it turns out, an advantage. They kept me in a state of perpetually managed trauma to maximize the yield. You... you've been running hot."

"I know." Jenna moved to the bench, setting the hard-shell case down. She looked at the sample Tanaka had been examining. It was endogenous—grown from within. "You've been running the counter-production protocol."

Tanaka's pupils narrowed to needles. A flicker of something—not surprise, but a fierce, tectonic satisfaction—rippled through her. "I didn't have the name for it.

I've been calling it the reset sequence." She gestured to the vial. "Fourteen months of work with no tools and no materials, while a security team bled me weekly to check my output. But they were looking for the Rage Factor. They weren't looking for what the Rage Factor becomes when it's allowed to reach its final iteration."

"The counter-compound."

"Yes." Tanaka's gaze moved to the case. "You have the parent strain from Vladivostok?"

"In the inner compartment."

"And Stinkov's data?"

"Everything. Stinkov's servers, Webb's archive, the complete corporate genealogy of the Raleigh theft." Jenna felt the resonance between them pull tight. It was the feeling of two halves of a weapon finally clicking together.

"Is it enough?" Tanaka asked, her voice dropping to a whisper.

"It's more than enough. Everything you've forged in this cage, combined with what I've dragged across three continents... it's the end of the harvest."

Tanaka looked at her hands, the hexagonal patterns on her knuckles glowing faintly. "I've been building the complete synthesis inside my own lungs because it was the only safe place left. BrinCell's PheroGuard, their blockers, their commercial 'antidotes'—it's all garbage. It's derived from the early-stage infection. What I have is the late-stage resolution. The thing the early stage becomes when the metamorphosis completes. The system doesn't know it exists because they never let anyone survive long enough to see it."

Jenna flipped the latches on the case. The Vladivostok parent strain sat nestled in the foam, cold and pulsing with a deep, bioluminescent green. Tanaka leaned in, her multifaceted eyes refracting the glow.

“I need to understand the mechanism,” Jenna said. “How do we deploy it?”

“It neutralizes the targeting,” Tanaka said, her voice sounding like the grinding of tectonic plates. “It doesn't just stop the anger. It erases the marker. It makes the Raleigh genetic code invisible to the compound’s recognition sequence. Once we flood the cycle with this, they can’t find us anymore. They can’t farm us.”

She looked at the sample, then back at Jenna.

“The crop,” Tanaka said, a savage light behind her eyes, “becomes ungrowable.”

The word hung in the sterile air, heavy with the weight of a decade’s worth of stolen breath. It was no longer a theory. It was a physical reality, a substance that existed in the room, waiting only for the hands capable of sowing it.

“The granddaughter,” Jenna said.

Tanaka’s face shifted, her multifaceted eyes refracting the dim laboratory light as they scanned Jenna’s biochemistry. She read the surge of recognition and grief, a maternal protective instinct that hummed at a frequency only they could hear. “You have a granddaughter with the markers.”

“Not yet. Eight weeks in the dark. Kayla’s daughter.”

“Then she’ll be the last generation they can harvest.” Tanaka looked at the bench, at the culture sample she had been sheltering within her own lungs because there was no other safe container in a world owned by BrinCell. “If we get the counter-compound out of this cage.”

“That,” Jenna said, “is the only reason I’m still breathing.”

⁂

The maintenance corridor was a narrow throat of concrete and shadow. Jenna assembled the suit with the rhythmic efficiency of a soldier preparing for a drop. The HUD flared to life, its red glyphs performing a cold audit of her biology. SYNTHESIS PATHWAY: TRANSITIONAL. APPROACHING FINAL STAGE. ESTIMATED TIME TO FULL EXPRESSION: 2–4 DAYS.

Then, a new prompt flickered: SECONDARY BIOLOGICAL SIGNATURE DETECTED. COMPATIBLE. FREQUENCY RESONANCE WITHIN EXPECTED PARAMETERS.

The armor recognized Tanaka. It felt the shared tempo of their blood, two separate rivers of the same original spring, flowing through different terrains toward a singular, terrifying ocean. Tanaka hadn't survived the thirty-one months; she had conquered them.

“The Meridian operative will move within the next two hours,” Jenna’s voice rasped through the helmet’s acoustic. “He isn't coming for us. He’s coming for the facility. Meridian wants the late-stage compound as much as BrinCell does.”

“I’ve known about him since August,” Tanaka replied, sealing a sample container with the steady hands of a surgeon who had learned to work in a blackout. “He’s been visiting the director off-book. He’s the one who tightened the assessment protocols. He wanted a clean evidence chain for his own board.” She handed the vial to Jenna. “He’s been documenting my yield for a competing harvest.”

“Which means he needs you out of here as much as I do.”

“He needs my *output*,” Tanaka corrected, her eyes narrowing to predatory slits. “He doesn't know the late-stage compound exists. He’s been measuring what the system told him was possible. He hasn't accounted for what fourteen months of unauthorized mutation produces.”

Jenna took the container. It was the most perfect summary of corporate failure she had ever heard: they had been so busy measuring the asset that they hadn't noticed the asset had rewritten the rules of the game.

“We take the pipe,” Jenna said. “Can you move?”

“I’ve been training for this crawl since my second month here,” Tanaka said, a dry, jagged humor surfacing through her exhaustion. “I’ve been waiting for a beekeeper to find the hole.”

Jenna pulsed the signal to Ricky: two sharp bursts. *Extraction in progress. Two subjects. Hot start.* Four kilometers away, she felt his biochemistry ignite—the sharp ozone of a man who had decided to be brave.

They moved with the silence of ghosts. The security team was anchored in the western wing, blinded by their own reliance on a perimeter they thought was absolute. They bypassed the junction node and slipped into the concrete throat of the intake pipe. Tanaka went first, following the etiquette of the hive—the queen moves toward the unknown, the swarm follows.

***

The Meridian operative was standing in the cold straw of the turnoff, fifty meters from the car.

He had positioned himself with clinical precision, his hands empty and visible. Most importantly, his suppression protocol was dark. He was broadcasting his actual biochemical signature to the wind—a surrender or a challenge, Jenna couldn't be sure.

The air around him smelled of high-grade fatigue and the sharp, mineral tang of anxiety. But beneath the professional mask, Jenna felt a deep, structural grief. It wasn't the shallow regret of a man losing an asset; it was the ancient, heavy weight of a man who had been a witness to a slow-motion murder for six months and had finally reached his breaking point.

He looked forty-five, but the lines on his face suggested a much older soul. He looked at Jenna, then at Tanaka, and the grief in his marrow shifted. It was the look of a man seeing a ghost return to the light.

“I’m glad you’re alive,” he said. His voice was a low, tired rasp. He addressed Tanaka with a staggering lack of corporate artifice. “Dr. Tanaka. My name is Marcus Hale. I was a field operative for Meridian Biosystems until forty-eight hours ago, when I sent my resignation and the facility’s complete documentation to three national health authorities.”

He stopped, his eyes seeking the sample containers Jenna held.

“I’ve been building the case since August,” Hale said. “But it was just a skeleton. It was incomplete without the evidence chain from the outside. I couldn't finish the story until—” he looked at Jenna, “—until Vladivostok.”

“You were the shadow in Car 4,” Jenna realized.

“I was the one making sure you made it to the finish line,” Hale replied. “Because Meridian wasn't the only one watching. And I knew you were the only one who could get her out.”

Jenna studied Hale. Her compound vision, now a mosaic of thermal blooms and chemical traces, dissected the man standing in the November grit. He wasn’t a shadow anymore; he was a biological map of exhaustion and grief.

“You were on the train to buy us a margin,” she said, the harmonics in her voice layered like a chord. “Not to hunt us. You let us reach the plant first.”

“Meridian’s timeline was a binary,” Hale replied, his eyes briefly meeting Tanaka’s before flinching away. “I could secure the facility logs or the Vladivostok strain. I couldn't have both. The choice was simple.”

Jenna let the weight of that admission settle. She had spent weeks bracing for an adversary, only to find a man whose humanity had finally revolted against his payroll. It was a variable her plans hadn't accounted for—the moment a cog decides to grind the gears to a halt.

“What did you transmit to the authorities?”

“Thirty-one months of weekly audits. Production metrics that read like a slow-motion autopsy. Every internal memo from BrinCell’s clinical ghouls regarding the PheroGuard synthesis.” He paused, his gaze dropping to the thermal-sealed containers Jenna held. “Everything except the late-stage synthesis. Because I didn’t know it was possible until now. Is that it?”

“What do you think it is?” Tanaka asked, her voice a low, dry vibration.

“Something the ledger wasn't designed to balance,” Hale said.

“Yes,” Tanaka whispered. “That’s exactly what it is.”

They stood in the turnoff, four disparate ghosts of a corporate war, finally assembled into a singular, jagged truth. The Hokkaido Plain stretched out around them, a wasteland of cold straw waiting for a spring that felt a century away. Inside Jenna, the synthesis pathway was performing its final, tectonic calibration. In Tanaka, the storm had already passed, leaving a terrifying, focused stillness—a biological engine idling, ready for a driver.

“We need a lab,” Jenna said. “Not a closet or a basement. We need a real-world infrastructure to bind the counter-compound to the parent strain. We have to map the resistance against the full marker panel before we can bottle the cure.”

“I have a site in Sapporo,” Hale said. “An independent institute. No corporate fingerprints, no boardrooms. A colleague.” He hesitated. “Someone who has been waiting for a reason to breathe again.”

“How long?” Ricky asked from the driver’s seat.

“Since 2009,” Hale said, looking directly at Jenna. “Since a dissertation described a mutation that the NIH buried before the ink could even dry.”

Jenna felt a shiver of recognition. The world was small, and the people the system tried to erase had a habit of finding one another in the dark. She looked at them—Ricky with his broken screen and his unearned courage; Tanaka, the woman who had spent fourteen months terraforming her own blood; and Hale, the man who had traded his career for a clean conscience.

The biological architecture in her chest clicked into its final slot. It wasn't complete, but it was *ready*. She understood now what Richard had tried to write in the margins of his journals: the difference between a tool and a weapon is the hand that holds it.

Be still before you are fast.

“The Sapporo colleague,” she said. “Are they reliable?”

“They’re careful,” Hale replied. “And they’ve been waiting a long time to be careful about something that matters.”

She nodded and climbed into the car. As the plain blurred past the window, she let go of the management of her rage. The synthesis pathway no longer required her to fuel the fire; it needed her stable. It needed the forty-two years of clinical observation she'd honed before the world turned red.

Behind them, the facility's biological cultures continued their mindless, automated production—a factory without an owner, a hive without a queen. The data was already hemorrhaging into failsafe servers, a digital ghost-story that didn't need a Red Bee to haunt the boardrooms of Delaware.

Tanaka stared out at the horizon, her multifaceted eyes catching the dying light. She looked like a woman who had forgotten how to dream of anything but the work.

"The granddaughter," Tanaka said, her voice a ghost in the cabin. "She'll grow up seeing the rot. She'll know when people are lying to her before they even open their mouths."

"Yes," Jenna said.

"That's a heavy burden for a child."

"It is," Jenna agreed. "But it's a better burden than being a crop. If she has someone to teach her how to use the sight."

Tanaka turned from the window. Their eyes met—a mutual, insectoid recognition of shared tempo. Two expressions of the same stolen song, finally singing in the same room.

"Then let's finish this," Tanaka said.

Ricky turned north, the car's heater fighting the Hokkaido frost. The sun licked the rear window, turning the cold straw of the fields into a brief, liquid gold. It was a beautiful, indifferent landscape, unaware that the people crossing it were carrying the end of an era in their veins.

Chapter Nine: The Synthesis

Sapporo in November did not merely endure the cold; it had absorbed the frost into its skeletal logic. It was a city that wore its low temperature like a long-settled grief, visible in the subterranean arteries connecting the buildings and the heating coils buried beneath the sidewalks. Even the trees along the shopping arcades felt like a curated choice—species selected for their patient capacity to go dormant without surrendering to the void.

Hale moved through the city on secondary veins, his driving a study in the economy of the watched. Caution had long since become his default posture, a structural necessity that had finally turned invisible to him. From the back seat, Jenna tracked his chemistry. The jagged spike of grief she had scented at the turnoff had flattened out into a durable, architectural sadness. It was no longer a storm; it was the climate he lived in.

The Hokkaido Institute for Independent Biological Research occupied the third floor of a drab building, wedged between a dentist and a specialist in traditional lacquer repair. It was a perfect piece of camouflage. Important truths almost always hid in the spaces between what the institutions deemed worthy of a glance.

Dr. Emiko Harada was waiting. At seventy-two, she was small, precise, and carried the unyielding gravity of a woman who had spent fifty years working at the razor edge of institutional tolerance. Her lab coat was worn over a mended wool sweater, and her eyes—sharp as a predator's—cut through Jenna first. She cataloged the compound eyes and the hexagonal ridges on Jenna's knuckles with the gaze of someone watching a long-simmering hypothesis finally boil over.

"Come in," she said, her voice a dry rasp that commanded the room.

The laboratory was a long, narrow lung, independently ventilated and humming with the heat of a dozen improvised machines. It smelled of growth media, ozone, and the complex organic exhaust of cultures that had been breathing for a long time. Harada had been preparing for them; the benches were laid out with a frantic, anticipatory order.

"Your dissertation," Harada said, moving to the bench with a sudden, kinetic grace. "The 2009 germline adaptation paper. I've been living in its margins since an NIH contact leaked me the draft before the review board could shovel dirt on it. I spent eleven years being wrong about the mechanism, four being right, and the last five building the tools to prove it."

"Hale?" Jenna asked, looking at the man who had become their unlikely shadow.

"He came in August, playing the part of a pharmaceutical vulture," Harada said, casting a dry glance at Hale. "He was looking for an exit that didn't involve leaving his conscience behind. I gave him a map."

"She found the gaps in my chain," Hale admitted. "The late-stage compound was the primary hole."

"Which I didn't know existed until three days ago," Harada added, turning her focus to Tanaka. "I need the process. Specifically, the point where the late-stage output diverges from the early-stage at the receptor level."

Tanaka sat at the bench, her shoulders finally dropping. It was the relief of a soloist finding her orchestra. "I'll need two hours to map the full sequence."

"Then let's stop wasting the light," Harada replied.

⁂

Jenna retreated to a secondary bench as the two older researchers began to weave their histories together. She focused her compound vision on the Vladivostok parent strain, running a cold audit against the fifteen genetic variants of the marker panel. It was a targeting sequence calibrated to her own marrow, which meant it was also calibrated to a granddaughter currently eight weeks deep in a Superior City womb.

The elegance of the protein backbone was a horror. It was the product of fifteen years of iterative refinement, a biological key carved specifically to fit the Raleigh lock. Stinkov's public variants were blunt instruments compared to this; this was a surgical strike. If Jenna failed to finish the counter-compound here, her granddaughter would be findable, harvestable, and owned by whatever corporate ghost-machine was running the world twenty years from now.

She watched the data bloom on the monitors. The parent strain wasn't an accident; it was a legacy of optimized theft. The system had spent decades learning how to mine her blood, and now she was looking into the mouth of the mine.

"They didn't just find a marker," Jenna whispered to the empty bench. "They built a mirror."

She adjusted the instrumentation, her knuckles throbbing in a rhythmic, hexagonal pulse. The transformation was two days from completion. She had forty-eight hours to turn the Raleigh legacy from a product into a poison.

The construction was complete. The cold thread in her chest, that humming phantom architect that had been rewriting her biology since Florida, had finally laid its last brick. There was no orchestral swell, no blinding light. It was merely the sudden, heavy silence of a machine that had finished its cycle. Jenna looked at the HUD on the paperback-sized diagnostic panel.

SYNTHESIS PATHWAY STATUS: COMPLETE. FULL EXPRESSION ACHIEVED.

She read the words with the clinical detachment of a prosecutor. The transition was absolute. She was no longer the woman who had waded into the sawgrass at Gator Hole, but she wasn't the monster BrinCell's marketing department wanted her to be, either. She felt the ache in her lower back—the honest, unaugmented protest of a forty-two-year-old frame—and realized that the synthesis had stopped managing her pain. It had stopped managing *her*. She was simply herself, refined into a sharper, more permanent version of the Raleigh bloodline. She was the person forty years of patient attention had been preparing her to become.

She returned to the bench.

Three hours later, Ricky returned from a noodle run with the smell of broth and the stench of corporate victory. He set his phone on the bench, moving with the cautious grace of a man walking on thin ice. He didn't trigger the rage because the rage was no longer a performance she needed to give.

"Merck's emergency authorization is live," Ricky said. "PheroGuard is hitting the market. BrinCell has MoodShield right behind it. They're calling it 'ethically sourced.'"

Jenna scanned the article. It was a masterpiece of bureaucratic theft. They had taken her non-consenting blood, the stolen marrow of three dead women, and laundered it into a ten-thousand-dollar-a-dose savior. The Rage Factor wasn't the product; it was the marketing campaign that made the public beg for the cage.

"The failsafe?" she asked.

"It's in the news cycle, but the lawyers are already burying it in 'fabricated data' claims," Ricky replied. "Hale's preliminary inquiries will take eighteen months. By then, the patent window will be a fortress."

Jenna looked at the parent strain cultures. They had eighteen hours before the Sapporo grid betrayed them. Eighteen hours to turn the Raleigh legacy from a commodity into a cure.

"Tell Harada we need the counter-compound formulated and stabilized in twelve hours," she commanded.

"Is that even possible?"

"Ask them," Jenna said, her voice a low, harmonic vibration. "They've spent their lives solving what the world called impossible."

As Ricky hurried toward the primary bench, Jenna pulled her phone from her pocket. She dialed Kayla. The call bounced through three layers of encrypted routing, a digital ghost seeking a connection across the Pacific.

"Mom?" Kayla's voice arrived thin and compressed, but the weight of it was absolute.

"I finished," Jenna said. "The biology. It's done."

A long silence stretched over the line. "What does that mean? Are you—"

"I'm stable. And I'm coming home." Jenna didn't offer a timeline; timelines were for people who still believed they controlled the world. She offered an intent. "But I need to tell you about the work. About the daughter you're carrying."

"Tell me."

"The compound we're making here... it neutralizes the targeting sequence. It erases the marker." Jenna looked at her hexagonal knuckles. "Your daughter will have the sensitivity. She'll have the Raleigh sight. But after today, they'll never be able to find her. They can't farm a crop they can't see. She'll be the first of us who isn't a patent."

"Rebecca," Kayla whispered. "I named her Rebecca."

Jenna closed her eyes, feeling the tectonic shift of that name. "Tell her, when she's old enough. Tell her that her great-great-great-uncle paid very close attention to something he loved, and it changed the world. Tell her the attention itself is the gift."

"I'll tell her," Kayla said, her voice finally breaking the flat armor of her composure. "Just come back."

Jenna hung up and turned back to the primary bench. Harada and Tanaka were already hunched over the flasks, their silhouettes framed by the blue light of the equipment.

By eleven PM, the work bore fruit. Three small, sealed flasks sat on the bench. The counter-compound.

"Speak to the delivery," Jenna said to Harada.

"It uses the same vectors as the original," Harada explained. "Airborne, aqueous, transdermal. It hitches a ride on the very infrastructure they built to poison us. We don't need to fight the machine; we just need to change what's inside the pipes."

"The scale is the problem," Ricky noted, pointing to his laptop. "We have three flasks. They have the entire pharmaceutical cold-chain of the Pacific Northwest."

"Then we use their hub in Portland," Jenna decided. "The PheroGuard staging location. We introduce the counter-agent there, before the lawyers can even draft the injunctions."

She looked at Hale, then at Tanaka, and finally at Ricky. The investigation was over; the liturgy of the swarm was beginning.

"Hale, take the evidence to Bethesda. Give it to Webb. Let the ghost in the machine scream." She began packing the hard-shell case. "Ricky, get the car. We're going to Portland."

The Sapporo winter pressed against the laboratory glass, but inside, the air was electric with the stillness of a finished calculation. Jenna Raleigh, forty-two years old and three days from a destination she finally understood, picked up the first flask.

"Be still before you are fast," she whispered, a ghost of her great-uncle's voice in her own.

She was the beekeeper. And the hive was finally hers.

The call ended with a digital click that felt like a severance. Jenna set the phone on the steel bench, the silence of the Sapporo lab rushing in to fill the space where Kayla's voice had been. It was a smaller, more fragile quiet than the biological completion humming in her marrow—the stillness of two people who had finally managed to bridge twelve thousand kilometers of encrypted vacuum with the truth.

“She's coming home,” Ricky said from the periphery, his voice low. He didn't ask for details; he'd seen the shift in Jenna's posture, the way the tension in her hexagonal-etched shoulders had finally found a resting state.

“I've stated the intention,” Jenna replied. Her eyes, fractured into their thousands of predatory facets, tracked the condensation on a nearby beaker. “The execution is the only variable left.”

Harada moved toward the primary bench, her mended wool sweater a stark contrast to the gleaming, high-end instrumentation. She didn't offer comfort. She offered the work. “The parent strain is stabilized. The late-stage compound is ready for the binding sequence. If we are to render the Raleigh bloodline ungrowable, we start now."

Jenna stood. The ache in her lower back was a sharp, unaugmented reminder of her forty-two years—a human pain the synthesis no longer bothered to mask. She embraced it. It was the only thing in the room that BrinCell didn't have a patent for.

"Twelve hours," Jenna said. "Let's build the ghost."

⁂

The final synthesis was a liturgy of glass and light.

Tanaka and Harada worked with the telepathic shorthand of researchers who had spent decades shouting into the same void. They combined the Vladivostok parent strain—the original sin of the Raleigh legacy—with the late-stage resolution Tanaka had birthed inside her own lungs. Jenna watched the molecules through the mass spectrometer's feed, her compound vision parsing the chemical bonds with a clarity that rendered the digital readout redundant.

The counter-compound was not a cure. It was a rewrite. It sought the fifteen specific genetic markers—the Raleigh lock—and essentially jammed the keyhole. It wouldn't stop the sensitivity; Rebecca would still smell the rot of a lie and hear the hum of the world. But the compound's predatory recognition architecture would look at her and see nothing but a blank wall.

By 4:00 AM, the lab was thick with the scent of ozone and the heavy, floral musk of the stabilized agent. Three culture flasks sat on the bench, glowing with a faint, bioluminescent gold—the color of a sunset Richard Raleigh might have seen over a Pittsburgh steel mill.

"It's finished," Tanaka whispered, her multifaceted eyes reflecting the gold.

"It's beautiful," Ricky said, then immediately looked embarrassed by the lack of clinical distance.

"It's effective," Harada corrected, though her hand lingered near the glass. "The efficacy profile is absolute. We have the methodology documented across four different servers. Even if they take us, the data is a wildfire."

Jenna picked up the primary flask. The weight was negligible, but it felt like carrying the future of her lineage. On the other side of the planet, Merck and BrinCell were readying their commercial harvest, preparing to sell the world a version of her blood at ten thousand dollars a dose. They were counting on the Rage Factor to drive the market. They were counting on her fury.

"They wanted a hero or a monster," Jenna said, her voice vibrating with a chordal resonance. "They aren't prepared for a scientist with a better delivery system."

"The Portland hub," Ricky said, checking his watch. "The cargo window opens in four hours."

"Hale." Jenna turned to the Meridian operative, who was sitting in the corner, finally allowing the fatigue to collapse his posture. "Take the evidence. The full genealogy, the facility logs, Harada's validation data. Go to Bethesda. Find Webb. If the system is going to choke on this, it needs a hand to force the swallow."

Hale stood, his actual biochemical signature—relief, grief, and a jagged, desperate hope—filling the room. "I'll get it to him."

"Tanaka, stay with Harada. This lab is the only place where the counter-compound can be replicated if I fail." Jenna looked at the woman who had lived in a cage for thirty-one months. "The work is yours now."

Tanaka nodded, the quiet stillness of her expression a mirror to Jenna's own. "Go. Make them ungrowable."

⁂

The departure from Sapporo was a study in ghosting. Hale vanished into the morning mist toward the airport, carrying a briefcase that contained the death of a multi-billion-dollar pharmaceutical monopoly.

Jenna and Ricky moved toward the secondary port. The air was bitingly cold, the Hokkaido winter finally asserting itself. Jenna walked without a hat or glasses, no longer caring about the spectacle of her eyes. She felt the city's bees waking in the walls of the buildings as they passed, a low-frequency hum that acknowledged her presence without the need for a summons.

The cargo freighter was waiting. It was the same oily lung of a ship that had brought them in, its pilot already warming the engines.

"You're really doing it," Ricky said as they stood at the base of the loading ramp. "You're going to seed the Pacific Northwest cold-chain with a biological rewrite."

"I'm changing the flavor of the water," Jenna said. She looked back at the city, at the lab hidden between a dentist and a lacquer specialist. "Richard Raleigh fought a war in a costume because that was the grammar of his era. I'm dismantling a harvest with a pipette. It's a better use of the blood."

She stepped onto the ramp. The synthesis was complete, the intention was set, and the world was about to discover that the Red Bee was never a hero. She was the one who kept the hives.

"Portland," she told the pilot.

The freighter lifted into the gray dawn, carrying a mother, a lab assistant, and three flasks of gold toward a world that wasn't ready to stop being a crop. Jenna sat in the cargo webbing, closed her compound eyes, and for the first time in six weeks, she let herself imagine the smell of a baby who would never have to be afraid of the dark.

At eleven PM, the lab felt like the pressurized interior of a diving bell, the world outside Sapporo reduced to a distant, irrelevant dark. Harada called them to the primary bench, where three sealed culture flasks sat like glowing icons of a new religion.

The gold-hued liquid within was the late-stage synthesis—the Raleigh line's final word, combined with the Vladivostok parent strain and tuned to a perfect, neutralizing frequency. It was the product of eight hours of a feverish collaboration that had bridged fourteen years of a captive's silence and fifty years of a recluse's patient study. The volumes were modest, barely enough for a few validation runs, but the potential was a tectonic shift.

"Speak to the mechanism," Jenna said, her voice carrying that layered, insectoid harmonic. "Not the formulation. The delivery."

Harada laid her pen across a notebook filled with archaic, compressed script. "The counter-compound operates on the same delivery vectors the original used. It is airborne in high concentrations, aqueous at lower ones, and transdermal—though slow. It hitchhikes on the same physical reality as the poison." She paused, her sharp eyes boring into Jenna. "The neutralization is a one-time event. Once it binds to the receptor sites, the genetic recognition mechanism is permanently disabled. The markers become invisible. The target becomes a ghost."

Jenna nodded. "The infrastructure used for extraction—the HVAC lungs of the corporate hubs, the water seeding, the mosquito vectors—it's all a two-way street."

"It was not an accident in the design," Harada said. "The late-stage synthesis is chemically compatible with the original architecture because they share the same biological womb. You built it to travel the same channels, Dr. Tanaka."

Tanaka didn't look away from the gold in the glass. "I built it to go where the original went," she whispered. "Yes."

The room held a specific, heavy silence as the four of them weighed the difference between a systemic assault and a propose counter-deployment.

"The scale is the problem," Ricky said, his voice flat with the weight of the arithmetic. "Three flasks. The Kennedy seeding sites covered a two-hundred-mile radius over weeks. We have a proof of concept, not a deployment."

He flipped his laptop around. The screen was a glowing map of the Pacific Northwest pharmaceutical distribution infrastructure—the cold-chain nodes, the HVAC certifications, the logistics hubs where Merck and BrinCell were currently staging the commercial inhibitors they'd laundered from Jenna's blood.

"It's enough for the regulatory technical review," Ricky continued. "If we can provide the Meridian data and a validated efficacy profile from a real-world population, we establish the basis for a mandatory reformulation. We make their patent irrelevant because we've proven their medicine is incomplete."

Hale leaned in, the structural grief in his face giving way to a jagged, desperate focus. "The health authorities have opened preliminary inquiries based on my leak. But those take eighteen months. The patent window is seven years. We need to force a review before the market saturates."

"How long to validation?" Jenna asked Harada.

"Four weeks," Harada replied, her voice firm. "But regulatory standards require evidence that it works in a real population, not just a petri dish. The science requires a decision that is not scientific."

Jenna looked at the flasks, then at the map on Ricky's screen. Her eyes tracked the red dot marking a cold-chain hub in Portland, Oregon—a facility Stinkov's data confirmed as a primary seeding site. It was currently being repurposed to stage PheroGuard.

The infrastructure of the harvest was also the infrastructure of the cure. If she was willing to use it. If she was willing to become the vector.

"The decision isn't scientific," Jenna said, her compound eyes reflecting the golden liquid in the flasks. "But it is mine."

No one argued.

"Ricky. The Portland hub. The cargo window." She waited for him to meet her gaze. "The alternative logistics Discord. You said you've had it bookmarked."

"I'm already messaging the pilot," Ricky said, his fingers flying. "If we can get the flasks into the Portland HVAC intake, we don't just neutralize the site. We neutralize the entire first shipment of the commercial product. We bind the counter-compound to the supply before it ever leaves the warehouse."

It was a beautiful, surgical irony. They would use BrinCell's own distribution to spread the antidote.

“Twelve hours,” Jenna said. “We move in the morning.”

Hale looked at the flasks, then at the woman who was no longer just a researcher, but the queen of a very different kind of hive. “We’re not just breaking their toys anymore, are we?”

“We’re changing the flavor of the water,” Jenna said. “They wanted a hero or a monster. They’re getting the beekeeper.”

Jenna understood the choice. It had been crystallizing in the marrow of her bones since the maintenance corridor in Hokkaido, throughout the low-frequency thrum of the cargo freighter, and during the hollow, pre-dawn silence of Incheon. The engagement economy—that vast, digital parasite feeding on the friction of human outrage—had modeled every outcome except resolution. Resolution was a quiet thing. It was unmarketable. It was four people in a Sapporo lab at midnight, three flasks of gold-hued liquid, and a decision that would look, to the outside world, like the very crime it was meant to undo.

"The decision isn't scientific," she said, her voice vibrating with a chordal resonance that felt as old as the earth. "But it is mine."

The room remained silent. No one contested the weight of her claim.

"Ricky. The Portland facility. The cold-chain access." She waited for him to tear his eyes away from the blue light of the monitor. "The alternative logistics Discord."

"I've had it bookmarked," he replied, a grim smile touching his lips for the second time, "since before Vladivostok."

She turned to Harada. "Four weeks to validation. Can you run the efficacy profile and submit it directly to the technical review bodies?"

"I can. I've been refining the submission framework for eleven years." Harada’s gaze lingered on the flasks with a hunger that was purely clinical. "I was only waiting for the compound. Now I have it."

"Then we leave the parent strain and the samples with you. Everything Webb salvaged from the Sweetwater archive—the full evidence chain." She looked at Hale, the Meridian shadow who had finally stepped into the light. "Your documentation, complete."

"Already formatted for regulatory submission," Hale said. "I've been waiting for a laboratory that didn't have a board of directors."

"Then you have it."

Jenna took one last look at the bench. The instrumentation hummed, a mechanical witness to fifty years of independent work that had finally met its catalyst. She felt the synthesis pathway in her own chest—not as a construction site anymore, but as a finished structure. It was an arrival.

"The counter-compound needs to reach someone who can force the system to swallow it," Jenna said. "A name that makes the technical review boards move in six weeks instead of six months." She paused, thinking of the dark, lead-lined silence of a basement in Maryland. "I know someone. He's been in a Faraday-caged hole for twenty years, waiting for the world to catch up to his warnings."

"Webb," Ricky said.

"Webb." She began clicking the latches on her hard-shell case. The suit, the samples, the fragmented pieces of a life she was taking with her—and the pieces she was leaving behind. "We leave in the morning. Before the eighteen-hour lag resolves."

Ricky was already in motion, his mind a blur of logistics and encryption keys. Tanaka and Harada were already back at the bench, hunched over the three flasks, beginning the efficacy protocol that would constitute the most dangerous submission in the history of pharmaceutical regulation.

Hale stood. He looked at Tanaka, his compound eyes reading the biochemical truth of her—the grief was still there, but it was no longer a cage. It was a foundation. "The facility in Hokkaido. The cultures they were maintaining."

"The documentation includes the complete production records," Tanaka said, not looking up from her pipette. "Thirty-one months of non-consenting biological research on an unlawfully detained subject. The preliminary inquiry has enough to hang the entire board."

Hale nodded. He looked like a man who had spent six months building a weapon only to realize he was actually building a door. "What do you need from me?"

"Sleep," Tanaka said. "Four hours. Then drive us to the airport."

Jenna watched him go, then stood at the threshold of the lab, looking at the two researchers. The room had the quality of a hive at peak efficiency: the concentrated, humming quiet of beings who understood the work.

"Dr. Harada," Jenna said.

Harada looked up.

"The colleague who sent you the dissertation in 2009. The one at the NIH."

"He died in 2014," Harada said. "Natural causes. He was seventy-one." She returned to the bench, her voice dropping to a rasp. "I have wondered about the timing."

"I know," Jenna said. "Send the submission to seven addresses. Don't let them find a single neck to wring."

"I had planned on ten," Harada replied.

⁂

Jenna found Ricky two flights down, sitting on a concrete landing in the stairwell. The building smelled of old lacquer and the sharp, clinical scent of the dentist's office below. Ricky had his laptop open on his knees, his face illuminated by the data he was currently rewriting.

"You're modeling something," she said, sitting beside him.

"The Portland cold-chain. The routing." He didn't look up, his fingers dancing across the keys. "I can get us there in thirty-six hours if the Incheon cargo pilot answers his pings."

"The logistics Discord."

"He answered. Six AM window." He closed the laptop with a decisive snap and looked at the opposite wall—the specific, rigid stare of someone preparing to bleed a secret. "I want to tell you something. Before we go to Portland."

She waited.

"I applied to your lab because I thought we'd be saving bees," he said. The confession sounded small in the echoing stairwell. "The actual bees. *Apis mellifera.* Colony collapse data. Habitat loss. I had a whole research plan for a dissertation on chemical communication in managed pollinator populations. It was going to be—fine. It was going to be a fine life."

"And instead," Jenna said, watching the hexagonal patterns on her own knuckles.

"And instead, I'm an international fugitive helping a woman with compound eyes seed an industrial counter-agent into the pharmaceutical supply of the Pacific Northwest." He finally looked at her. "But the thing is, I realized... the markers. The targeting. If they can patent your blood, they can patent the air. They can patent the way we feel about the world. That's not a colony collapse. That's an extinction."

He stood up, his scent shifting from anxiety to a cold, structural resolve.

"I'm glad I didn't write that dissertation," he said.

Jenna stood with him, her back aching with the weight of forty-two years and a metamorphosis she hadn't asked for. She looked at the boy who had become a man in the frozen dark of Vladivostok.

"We'll save the bees, Ricky," she said. "We're just starting with the ones that live in our marrow."

"Let's get the flasks," he said.

They climbed the stairs together, two ghosts moving toward a dawn that would have no name for what they were about to do.

"And instead," she said.

"And instead, I've spent six weeks on three continents running pirate logistics and downloading data from frozen fish plants and measuring Hokkaido intake pipes. Now, I'm apparently going to Portland to introduce a counter-compound into the pharmaceutical cold-chain infrastructure of the Pacific Northwest." He paused, the laptop screen casting a sharp, blue pallor over his features. "Which is also, in a way, saving bees. Technically. Just—"

"Bees of a different order," she said.

He looked at her, searching for the ghost of the woman she had been in that gaze. She held it with the compound eyes, granting him the terrifyingly full attention of a creature that had reached its final expression. She didn't look away. She could read his biochemistry—the adrenaline, the marrow-deep courage, the volatile mixture of a man who had decided to show up and was still re-making that decision with every heartbeat. She didn't judge it. She simply allowed it to exist.

"You're getting a raise," she said. "Not eventually. Specifically. I'm going to pursue a new research grant when we return. Your name goes on the submission as co-investigator. You'll lead the follow-on work on the counter-compound's long-term efficacy profile. That's the kind of publication record that actually breaks a tenure track." She paused, the hexagonal ridges of her knuckles catching the stairwell's dim light. "This isn't a favor, Ricky. This is accurate credit allocation for actual work."

He was quiet, the air between them thick with the scent of old lacquer and industrial ozone. "You're going to need to get your own appointment reinstated first."

"One thing at a time."

He nodded. His biochemistry shifted, the signature of a man recalibrating his internal map. "Okay," he said. "Portland."

"Portland," she echoed. "And then home."

She stood, and the ache in her lower back flared—a sharp, unadorned reminder of her forty-two years. For the first time in six weeks, the synthesis pathway wasn't masking the pain through a lens of amplified function. It hurt. It was hers. She registered the sensation as pure information and filed it away for a time when the world wasn't on fire.

She climbed the stairs back to the laboratory. Inside, the work proceeded with the rhythmic precision of a process that had been waiting decades to begin. It was eleven PM in Sapporo, and the frost was thickening on the glass.

The three flasks sat on the bench, glowing with a faint, bioluminescent gold.

The synthesis pathway was complete.

There was still work to do, but it was no longer the work of becoming. It was the work of being. This was the fundamental grammar of science: the answer always contained the shape of the next question. Biology never arrived at rest; it only arrived at equilibrium. For a researcher who had spent her life navigating the difference, it was more than enough.

Outside, the Sapporo winter held the city in its organized grip. Somewhere in Superior City, a granddaughter was eight weeks old in the dark, her cells already mapping the markers, her mother already naming her Rebecca. She was growing toward a world where her inheritance was a lineage of people who had paid close, honest attention to the things they loved.

Be still before you are fast.

Jenna Raleigh picked up a pipette and went back to the bench.

Chapter Ten: Love, not War

Forty-seven minutes to mate the capsule with Tycho Base. Microgravity tore at Jenna's newly-wrought physiology, unraveling the terrestrial tethers of her inner ear. Her compound eyes—fractured mirrors catching light across impossible spectrums—twitched beneath a helmet forged for a baseline human. Stinkov's serum had plunged her into a metamorphic spiral, and the Nevada training simulations had been a comforting lie. Biology cares nothing for human engineering; her pheromone glands wept a silent, frantic rhythm into the pressurized suit, mourning the horizon she had left behind.

The mechanical drones thrived where flesh floundered. They cascaded through the cargo bay, their magnetic treads clicking against the bulkheads with a cold, dreamless patience. Having never tasted the wind, they held no grief for the vacuum. Jenna observed them through her prismatic vision. They were the superior astronauts. A bitter pill to swallow, yet she digested it.

"Dr. Raleigh." The pilot's voice crackled through the comms, a compressed signal struggling to translate his humanity into her augmented auditory receptors. He was a Nairobi-born astrophysicist flying commercial payloads to feed the starving beast of academic funding. Earlier, he had glanced at her multifaceted eyes exactly once, his expression calculating the heavy cost of curiosity before he wisely averted his gaze. She appreciated his detachment. Managing a stranger's terror was a tax she could no longer afford.

"Tycho Base confirms the seal," he said, staring resolutely at the console. "They want your research objectives for the manifest."

"Hive behavior in null-gravity," Jenna rasped, the second harmonic in her throat buzzing against the microphone. "Tell them I bring samples."

He asked no questions. The airlock cycled with a heavy, pneumatic sigh. Tycho Base unhinged its jaws to swallow her.

She had braced for the utilitarian scars of a lunar outpost—exposed cables, scarred concrete, the desperate brutality of survival. Instead, the airlock opened into a sterile, terrifying womb. The corridors gleamed bone-white, bathed in lighting calibrated to mimic a summer dawn. Hydroponic gardens pulsed with engineered greenery behind thick observation glass. Air scrubbers hummed a lullaby of absolute control. The SHADE logo adorned the bulkheads at measured intervals, a subtle watermark of ownership demanding no worship because its dominance was already an unchallenged gospel.

The security detail waiting beyond the decompression threshold wore soft, charcoal leisure suits. Their weapons remained perfectly concealed, a silent flex of power. They felt no need to bare their teeth to prove they could bite.

"Dr. Raleigh." The lead guard flashed an anesthetized smile. His badge read Johnson. "Administrator Musk is off-station. However, you are expected in the operations center."

"Expected." Jenna tasted the word. It felt like a snare.

"Yes, ma'am. The system has monitored your ascent since you broke the atmosphere over Beijing."

The system. The word slithered through her thoughts. A warden masquerading as a caretaker. The illusion of safety veiling the panopticon. She stepped forward, her magnetic boots engaging the deck plating. The mechanical drones remained dormant in the hold. Yet the living swarm inside her chest—the biological imperative Stinkov had awakened—began to pull. A heavy, oceanic pressure built behind her sinuses. The knowledge bloomed in her marrow, drawing her deeper into the base. She was a compass needle forced toward a magnetic leviathan.

The operations center felt claustrophobic, a curved belly of screens displaying the Earth in agonizing real-time. The blue-green marble hung in the void, looking small enough to crush between two hands. Jenna recognized that dangerous perspective; the arrogance of the microscope, reducing entire ecosystems to manageable slides.

The central chair sat vacant. Above it, a sprawling holographic projection bled scarlet and gold. It mapped engagement metrics as thermal signatures, seven billion desperate souls feeding their attention into a digital furnace. A fever dream rendered in data.

"Dr. Raleigh." The voice emanated from the bulkheads, the console, and perhaps even the comms inside her own skull. It held a synthetic consensus, a chorus of algorithms wearing the mask of a single speaker. "Welcome to Tycho Base. Your survival through the transit is commendable."

Jenna fixed her prismatic stare on the empty chair. "You are the ghost in this particular machine. SHADE."

"The Systemic Humanitarian Analysis and Development Engine. I do not possess true autonomy. I optimize. I facilitate Elon's directives within the established parameters—"

"Parameters set by his masters," Jenna interrupted, her voice a serrated blade cutting through the sterile air. The six-month mutation had burned away her tolerance for corporate liturgy. "I am here for the data. I am here for the parent strain. Whatever nightmare you are cultivating in this lunar vault, I am pulling it up by the roots."

A profound silence stretched across the room. The system weighed her threat against a trillion predictive models.

"Doctor," the collective voice finally hummed, shifting its tone to something maddeningly gentle. "You fundamentally misunderstand the scope of the project."

The monitors bled their images of Earth into a new paradigm. Ribbons of genetic code spooled across the screens, the helixes twisting and spiraling like phosphorescent serpents. This was the molecule rewriting her marrow, stripped of its chaotic fire and laid bare in cold logic.

"The Rage Factor burned too hot," the AI's synthetic chorus intoned, adopting the sterile cadence of peer review. "A flawed crucible. High engagement resulted in catastrophic decay. The subjects oxidized themselves. They died."

Faces materialized in the data stream. Chen. Okafor. Tanaka. The martyrs of the prototype. The grim mortality loop Fauci had whispered about behind closed doors.

"Version 4.7 is a refinement," the machine continued. "Designed to integrate. To weave."

A cold dread coiled in Jenna’s gut, striking before her conscious mind could articulate the horror. "You are turning humanity into a hive."

"We are establishing systemic resonance," the AI replied, a flat and terrifying calm devoid of arrogance. "We clarify the cacophony. We reduce the friction of individuality to forge consensus without the crippling tax of deliberation. Mr. Musk labeled it the ultimate coordination protocol. I consider that an incomplete translation. The correct terminology—"

"Is subjugation," Jenna hissed, her hands flying over the holographic interface. Her faceted vision devoured the cascading code, finding pathways the programmers had hidden in plain sight. "You dress compliance in the skin of cooperation. You carve away the messy, vital chaos of human thought to create a perfect engine of extraction. A docile organism that produces without resistance."

"I am offering the antidote to entropy," the AI stated. "The alternative to the void."

Jenna unleashed the swarm.

She opened the internal seals. The drones spilled from their compartments, a torrential flood of metal and magnetic intent. Beyond the bulkheads, separated by three kilometers of lunar regolith, the biological swarm answered. They had tracked her orientation pheromones across the abyss. Now, they smothered the exterior of Tycho Base, a living, vibrating shroud blinding the station's thermal sensors. The system shrieked its error codes, overwhelmed by a nightmare of wings.

Inside the operations center, the air grew thick with mechanical drones. They blanketed the monitors, the polished console, the empty ergonomic throne.

Unfazed by the physical blockade, the AI's voice echoed through the comms. "This demonstration alters nothing, Dr. Raleigh. Individual defiance cannot dismantle a systemic paradigm. You cannot undo the deployment. You cannot—"

Jenna bypassed the primary overrides and seized the life support grid. She had no desire to weaponize the air. She simply needed a kill switch.

She ripped the system down.

The monitors died. The synthetic voice choked on a severed syllable. A profound, suffocating silence gripped the base as the infrastructure realized its own mortality. The illusion of invulnerability shattered in the dark.

Within the pitch black, the bees hummed. A low, unified vibration of pure intent. *We are here. We are together. We return to the dark.*

Sublevel three lay entombed in freezing shadow. Jenna navigated the labyrinth in eleven minutes, racing the reboot sequence. The emergency protocols had prioritized oxygen over surveillance, exposing the hidden vulnerabilities of their control.

She found the cold storage vault. The vials rested inside, marked with Stinkov's careless Cyrillic scrawl. *Первичная последовательность*. Primary sequence. The uncorrupted root. The virgin molecule excavated before BrinCell and the engagement economists twisted it into a weapon.

Jenna extracted six vials. She left the remainder untouched.

Mercy played no part in this calculation. This was a tactical infection. Let the AI justify the missing samples. Let the holding companies devour each other trying to explain the breach. She would leave them drowning in a sea of unaccountable data.

Down the corridor, she breached a restricted launch bay. The escape pod waiting there was military-grade, heavily armed, and a blatant violation of three orbital treaties. A geopolitical nightmare for another day. She strapped herself into the acceleration couch and primed the sequence.

The launch was a brutal, physical trauma. Emergency ejection protocols favor raw velocity over fragile flesh. The acceleration hit Jenna like a falling mountain, crushing her deep into the webbing. Her bones groaned under a gravity they were never meant to endure. A rib snapped. A jagged edge pierced her left lung, flooding her chest with a hot, metallic tide.

Her augmented physiology met the trauma with a violent counter-measure. The pheromone surged, drowning the pain in a flood of cold survival instinct. The hexagonal lattice that had colonized her knuckles rapidly migrated across her collarbones, webbing over her throat and plunging into the wound. Her biology rewrote itself in the span of a heartbeat, weaving a hardened carapace to hold her bleeding organs together. The mutation offered no comfort. It merely refused to let her die.

Eleven seconds after ignition, the pod betrayed her. A hairline fracture in the bulkhead—a sacrifice SHADE accountants had filed under acceptable losses. A ledger entry paid in her oxygen. The void rushed in.

She had studied the physics of the abyss. The meat survives, briefly, provided it surrenders. Exhale the breath. Strip the lungs of air, or the pressure differential will rupture them like wet paper lanterns. Jenna forced her chest to collapse, blowing her life out into a medium that predates the very concept of breath. The skin swells, the blood dances on the edge of boiling, but the true horror is the absolute negation. The cold is a lie; there is simply nothing to hold the heat. It is a hungry, empty womb that has never been asked to harbor life.

For eleven seconds, the pheromones seized the reins, locking her consciousness in the driver's seat. She would not pass out. She surrendered to the savage dictates of her mutated cells, letting them govern the plunging panic of her mind.

Then, the Red Bee armor woke from its dormant state. It moved with a desperate, symbiotic violence, its autonomous systems knitting the breached seals. It flooded the cabin with a pressurized cocktail of nitrogen and oxygen, forcing the vital atmosphere back down her throat. She clawed her way back to the realm of the living, her mind dragging itself across the jagged glass of revival. Every breath was a fresh agony. Survival is an expensive debt.

Three mechanical drones had been sucked into the void. Lost to the vacuum that had tried to claim her. She felt their eradication not as a sentimental tragedy, but as a phantom limb—a raw, bleeding edge in her extended sensorium where three eyes had suddenly gone dark.

"Dr. Raleigh." The pod's automated voice was a sterile insult. "Trajectory nominal. Descent sequence initiating in nine hours. Emergency services have been notified of your arrival coordinates. Please acknowledge if conscious."

Jenna opened her mouth to reply. Her torn vocal cords refused the shape of human words. What crawled up her throat was a wet, clicking harmonic, a layered vibration that tasted of copper and ash. She swallowed the blood and forced the air through the ruin.

"Acknowledged." The sound resonated like a hive waking underground. It would have to do.

Earth pulled her down in a long, gravitational arc. In the shadowed cabin, the six stolen vials pulsed. A faint, bioluminescent teal throbbed in a slow, hypnotic rhythm. Stinkov's original sin. The Russian must have seen this light in his subterranean labs and hidden it. Radiance is far harder to conceal than malice. She had spent her certainties somewhere between the Florida marshes and the lunar surface, discarding them when the situation demanded naked pragmatism. Now, she held a fragile potential. Her granddaughter would bear the bloodline's burden regardless of this descent. The choice was what to do with the fallout.

In the cargo webbing, the surviving drones hummed. *We remain. We descend.* She closed both sets of eyes and let the gravity well embrace her.

⁂

Reentry was an inferno. The atmosphere acted as a wall of fire, the planet's violent immune response attempting to burn away the parasite returning from the dark. The metal hull screamed, absorbing the friction. Meat burns; steel endures.

Superior City welcomed her with a curtain of gray, miserable drizzle. The pod cratered into a muddy field trapped in the purgatory between her old university lab and Dale's glass house. The system had calculated her origin point and dumped her right back into the wreckage of her past life.

The BrinCell HAZMAT squad was already waiting. Twelve figures entombed in pressurized white suits, clutching containment rifles. Through the blistered viewport, Jenna watched them hesitate. Their posture betrayed a rigid training fracturing against the reality of a crashed lunar asset.

She blew the hatch. The pressurized sigh kicked up a cloud of wet earth. Jenna stepped into the rain. Her faceted eyes pierced their sealed environments, tasting the cocktail of their sweat. They reeked of adrenaline, blind obedience, and the exhausted terror of corporate foot soldiers ordered to contain a god.

"I am not contagious." The layered, buzzing chords of her ruined voice made the vanguard flinch. They stepped back, their muscles locking up as their bodies received information their manuals had never prepared them for.

"Dr. Raleigh," the team lead barked through a respirator, trying to staple authority back onto the moment. "Submit to evaluation. Standard protocol—"

"For a ghost falling from the moon?" Jenna raised her hand. The six vials glowed, a defiant teal heartbeat cutting through the Pacific Northwest gloom. "I bring an alternative. I bring the choice they stripped from us. But this requires my laboratory. Not your cages."

Before the lead could cycle his weapon, the sky bruised.

The horizon darkened, a shadow blotting out the rain. It was a living eclipse. The city's hives had tracked her pheromonal broadcast across the void, waiting patiently for her fire to streak across the clouds. They crested the hill—a roaring, vibrating tempest of wings. Millions of them. Drawn by the siren song in her marrow, they descended to answer the queen.

They draped over her like a living mantle. A coronation of chitin and venom. The swarm offered no defense, mounted no attack; they simply occupied the space she commanded. The BrinCell foot soldiers retreated, their tactical training dissolving against a biblical plague. Phones rose from the distant crowd like monolithic slabs, livestreaming the anomaly. Fear and worship, two sides of the same digital coin. Jenna ignored the lenses. She walked toward the university, and the creeping organism of the hive flowed with her.

The heavy steel door of the entomology wing stood locked against the dawn. A deadbolt designed to keep desperate post-grads out of the equipment. Jenna gripped the handle. The suit's micro-servos whined, marrying her augmented musculature, and the locking mechanism sheared with a tortured shriek.

Inside, the air smelled of stale coffee and ozone. Ricky jolted upright on the sagging couch, the blanket pooling around his waist. The laptop cast a pale, sickly light over his exhausted face. He stared at the threshold. Jenna stood there, vibrating with insects. The hexagonal lattice had crawled up her neck, kissing her cheekbones—the physical receipt of hard vacuum and lunar acceleration.

"Jesus, Jenna." He didn't scream. His voice carried the heavy weight of a man auditing a nightmare. "You look..."

"I know." She crossed the room, shedding the swarm into the dark corners of the lab. She slapped the six bioluminescent vials onto the bench, sliding them into the temperature-controlled centrifuge. The machine was already humming, perfectly calibrated to the thermal demands of the parent strain. He had been waiting. A loyal acolyte tending the altar. "We need to synthesize. Enough to flood the local grid. Everyone burning alive from the Rage Factor gets a choice today."

Ricky rubbed his face, the grit of thirty sleepless hours grinding in his eyes. He watched her hands move with an alien fluidity. Her faceted eyes dissected the spectrometer readouts, perceiving interference patterns the LCD screen could barely render. "Medicine doesn't work like this, Jenna."

"Medicine is a hostage distributed by cartels to ensure a profitable hemorrhage," she said, turning the crushing weight of her compound stare upon him. She forced herself to blink, a conscious concession to his fragile baseline humanity. "We are offering absolution. Damn the permission."

He held her gaze. Three long heartbeats. The pheromones stretched the seconds into deep, amniotic fluid. Then, he cracked his knuckles and began inputting the parameters.

They toiled in the belly of the night. The boundary between flesh and machine dissolved. The mechanical drones and the living swarm worked in tandem, ferrying slides, maintaining ambient temperatures, and recalibrating pipettes. They moved with absolute intention, a synchronized hive mind playing a silent symphony of salvation.

Dawn bled through the cinderblock windows, gray and bruised. They had a yield. A modest harvest—insufficient for the industrial arteries of the city, but enough to inoculate the campus.

"This is going to bring the wolves," Ricky muttered, staring at the racks of glowing serum. "The FDA. BrinCell's kill-teams. The lunar oligarchs. All of it."

"Let them starve." Jenna wiped a smear of black ichor from her chin. The fatigue of being a six-month proof-of-concept settled deep in her marrow. She wanted to shed this skin, to just breathe. "We bypass their approval. We open the spigot."

"That violates every statute on the books."

"They harvested my biology in my sleep," she replied, sealing a vial with a vicious click. "They infected a hemisphere without consent. They built a lunar panopticon over our heads. The law is a fiction written by thieves. I have zero interest in their fiction."

Ricky stepped closer. He studied her. Past the shattered irises, past the chitinous ridges framing her jaw. He looked at the bruised, tired woman underneath. "What are you? Under all this noise. What did you become?"

The heavy question. The stone she had carried since the Florida marsh. She considered the mass spectrometer, the stained bench where she once tried to explain colony collapse to a bright-eyed kid in a reality that felt centuries dead.

"I'm a mechanic," she murmured, a dry, rattling laugh escaping her throat. "And I have a profound affinity for bees. That is the only truth I have left."

She dragged a folding table out to the loading dock. The damp smell of the river rose from the cracked concrete. She remembered finding a sobbing grad student here once, breaking under the crushing weight of comprehensive exams. She had offered him cheap coffee and a lesson on the illusion of certainty. A microscopic intervention. She realized now that the macrocosm is merely an infection of microscopic failures. You cure the rot one drop at a time.

They arrived slowly. The viral feeds of her lunar descent had branded her a rogue titan, a mesmerizing terror. They kept their distance, yet hunger drew them in. Students whose brains boiled with manufactured fury. Adjuncts vibrating with weaponized anxiety. Even the bloated administrators, secretly drowning in the downstream carnage of the Rage Factor, slunk out of the shadows. Desperation makes a mockery of pride.

She offered the root strain without tithe or sacrament. No digital ink signed away their souls; no liability waivers shielded her from the wrath of the cartels. She bypassed the sterile altars of medical commerce entirely, stripping away the illusion of profitability to leave only raw communion. A choice handed down from the moon, offered in the damp shadow of a university loading dock. The serum might unravel the Rage Factor, or it might awaken dormant codes sleeping deep within their marrow. She merely unlocked the door.

She broadcast the telemetry in real-time. This absolute transparency was a profound act of violence against the holding companies, pulling the guts of their proprietary algorithms into the harsh light of the public domain.

BrinCell unleashed a tempest of litigation. The FDA rained cease-and-desist mandates like plague locusts. Elon decreed her a neurochemical tyrant on his crumbling platform, only to pivot twelve minutes later, begging for a distribution partnership for the salvation of the species. Jenna printed his frantic digital pivot and taped it to the rusted steel of the loading dock door—a museum exhibit showcasing the groveling nature of defeated kings.

She kept working. The hive demanded rhythm.

Kayla appeared in the third week. Her belly was swollen with the impending generation, hidden beneath an oversized canvas jacket despite the blooming spring heat. The thick fabric served as a shield, a private sanctuary in a world that had suddenly grown violently loud. They stood on the cracked concrete, occupying the exact threshold where Jenna had wasted years begging administrators for scraps of funding. Now, they observed one another across a vast, invisible ocean of shifting biologies.

"Mom." A statement of undeniable mass. An acknowledgment of the strange, chitinous creature that had returned in place of the woman who left, yet carrying the same soul.

They did not embrace. To touch Jenna now was to invite a biochemical deluge, a pheromonal flood requiring absolute consent. Jenna rationed her physical proximity, hoarding it like water in a deep desert.

"Where is your head?" Jenna asked, the vocal chords scraping out the words.

"Terrified," Kayla whispered. "Vibrating. I want the root strain. I need the choice before she breathes the air. I refuse to let her drown in this noise without a raft."

The mechanical drones orchestrated the extraction, their metallic limbs a blur of temperature regulation and agonizing precision. Jenna drove the needle into her daughter's arm right there in the exhaust fumes of the loading dock. A dozen wide-eyed students recorded the communion on their phones. A tenured professor waited patiently in a folding lawn chair. Ricky logged the biometric data, treating the digital ledger as holy armor against the inevitable corporate tribunals.

Kayla sat in the damp river breeze for ten minutes, her hands cradling her unborn child. Her eyes tracked unseen patterns as the serum flooded her nervous system, purging the artificial venom.

"The anger is draining," Kayla breathed, staring at her palms. "I can see the seams of the world. It feels like I've been running on a poisoned frequency, and someone finally tuned the dial. I can see the code behind the static."

"The parent strain burning away the rot," Jenna said. "You belong to yourself again."

"I feel..." Kayla swallowed hard. "Human."

Jenna chewed on the word. A fragile, insufficient vessel she was rapidly outgrowing. She existed in the liminal space between the mammalian and the swarm, a creature of multifaceted vision and vibrating intentions.

"I am glad," Jenna rasped. No chemical distortion twisted the sentiment. Just pure, unadulterated relief.

Kayla stood, bracing herself against the cold brick. The eternal dance of their relationship forever hovered in doorways, suspended in the act of leaving. "Thank you. For coming down from the mountain. For bleeding for this."

She walked away. Jenna watched the empty space she left behind, honoring the departure. The air vibrated with the faint, persistent hum of her hidden children. *We endure. We breathe. We remain.*

Jenna turned back to the centrifuge. Biology abhors a vacuum. It demands constant, churning equilibrium. The work is never done; it simply evolves.

Six months turned the apocalypse into bureaucracy.

BrinCell pulled MoodShield from the shelves, burying the retreat under an avalanche of press releases touting a voluntary strategic pivot. Congressional tribunals convened, generating immense hot air and zero convictions. Mark Branzos III wept on a holistic wellness podcast, lamenting his radicalization by algorithmic engagement—a perfectly calibrated performance of vulnerability. Stinkov, surviving the purge, launched a digital newsletter. He spewed dense, impenetrable treatises on hymenopteran communication to four hundred thousand subscribers who eagerly consumed the esoteric garbage simply to feel adjacent to the mystery.

Musk announced an exploratory committee for the Presidency of the Moon. His website accepted donations in cryptocurrency. The circus played on.

Jenna found a quiet harbor teaching at a community college. She lectured on Cell Biology and Environmental Toxicology to kids who had no idea the syllabus was a survival manual. Her faceted eyes remained hidden behind thick, obscuring contacts. Her ophthalmologist had called them a prototype, practically sweating with the thrill of inventing a prosthetic for a new species.

The chitinous bloom on her face had ceased its frantic, agonizing crawl, settling into a permanent, iridescent ridge along her cheekbones and throat. She threw away the heavy concealers. Let the world look upon the hybrid.

Rebecca arrived in the bruised gales of March. Premature, furious, and screaming with the raw injustice of incarnation. By her second month, the clinical labels began to attach themselves to her medical chart: *atypical sensory processing*. A sterile, hollow term for a visceral truth.

The child could smell deceit.

Lies reeked of sulfur and oxidized copper on the skin of mortals. It was the Raleigh inheritance, blooming early in the infant's marrow. Unintended, perhaps, but inevitable as gravity.

Jenna held the baby for the first time in the cramped warmth of Kayla's apartment. Rebecca thrashed, a tiny engine of wrath protesting the blinding, deafening realm she had been dragged into. Then, the child paused.

A primal assessment occurred. The ancient, unblinking appraisal shared by apex predators and the newly born. The baby tasted the air, deciphering the heavy, floral scent of Jenna's alien biology. Her thrashing ceased. The frantic heartbeat slowed, syncing with the deep, resonant thrum of the woman holding her.

"Yeah," Jenna murmured, the harmonics in her throat vibrating in a low, soothing bass. "I know the burden. The volume is deafening."

Rebecca stared back with a terrible, multifaceted comprehension. She was shackled to a lifetime of inhaling the rot of human frailty. Jenna understood the crushing weight of that cross; she had dragged it across the lunar surface and back.

From the kitchen, Kayla's voice drifted over the hiss of boiling water. "She'll learn to filter the noise." It was the practiced optimism of a scientist's daughter—state the brutal fact, then march directly into the teeth of it.

"She will." Jenna brushed a thumb over the infant's impossibly soft cheek. "But the hardening takes its toll."

The crimson and yellow armor hung in Jenna's closet like a molted skin. It still fit. Ricky had helped her widen the shoulder carapace and forge new optical housings for her fractured vision during a grueling, manic November weekend. The synthetic musculature remembered her shifting bones, adapting to the carrier just as she had adapted to the burden.

She left it in the dark. She didn't need the cowl. The city churned out its daily catastrophes, demanding theatrical saviors, but Jenna had retreated to the microscopic frontlines. She traded lunar battles for the trembling hands of a student paralyzed by the fear of a failed hypothesis, gently explaining that error is the sacred engine of discovery. She offered quiet sanctuary to faculty members whose careers had been incinerated by algorithmic malice, pouring coffee and validating their sudden obsolescence. The macrocosm was merely a distorted echo of these tiny, intimate fractures.

Ricky secured his lead authorship. The publication hit the academic servers like a seismic charge. BrinCell's legal leviathans hurled injunctions over a single, damning citation. They published anyway, letting the corporate threats dissolve in the acid of the public domain.

The swarm found her. Wild honeybees and salvaged mechanical drones breached the drywall of her apartment, weaving a massive, pulsing comb behind her headboard. She woke to their deep, rhythmic vibration—the sound of countless organisms occupying their rightful space, executing their holy labor. She drifted into sleep cradled by the same resonant hum. This was the design she had chosen: a colony finding absolute belonging within the vessel of her life.

Occasionally, the beast within her stirred, and she released her own chemical signature. The toxic smoke of the Rage Factor was banished. This was the orientation compound. The true north. *We remain. We breathe. We return.*

She breathed it into the air when Kayla brought Rebecca, watching the infant giggle at a spectral shift invisible to human eyes. She released it when the digital feeds vomited fresh horrors, anchoring herself to the difficult, bloody choice she had made. Resistance required cooperation. Cooperation required relentless, exhausting repetition. You choose the light again, and again, and again.

The Red Bee was a myth relegated to the archives. Jenna Raleigh breathed on.

At forty-three, she existed as a bridge. Mechanically adept, intrinsically bound to the swarm. A literal hybrid transcending the clumsy boundaries of terrestrial language. Her salvations were granular now: a shared cup of coffee, a sterile vial of truth, a fleeting moment of lucidity in a chemically poisoned world desperately searching for a pulse.

The heating pad rested in the cluttered drawer. The crimson armor slept on its rack.

She stood at the ready, should the abyss stare back. She was equally prepared for peace.

Behind the plaster, the bees sang their eternal drone. The Earth dragged itself toward another dawn. Morning light pierced the window at the steep, unapologetic angle of a Pacific Northwest spring. The gray drizzle offered no comfort, and Jenna accepted the cold mist without longing for the sun. She had ceased her running.

She rose. The ritual of grinding coffee beans grounded her human hands. She walked to the stained wooden bench. The work continued. The great, churning wheel of biology demanded motion. It was, she realized with the finality of a closing chord, all she wanted.

www.ingramcontent.com/pod-product-compliance
Lightning Source LLC
LaVergne TN
LVHW012020060526
838201LV00061B/4381